The Holden House

HOLDEN HAUNTINGS, BOOK 1

EMMA LEIGH REED

ELR PUBLISHING

Holden House

By

Emma Leigh Reed

Books by E.L. Reed

Memories of Murder Series

Hatchet

Spikes

Poison

Dagger

Books by Emma Leigh Reed

A Fine Line

A Time to Heal

Second Chances

Trusting Love

Mirrrored Deception

The Rules Series

Making the Rules

Breaking the Rules

Prologue

Tonight was her first wedding anniversary. Cecilia's heart broke as she reflected on the past year. Brandon Stafford had been her true love, and she had been ecstatic at the thought of her parents arranging their marriage. Although he was a decade older than her, at her tender age of nineteen, she was excited to start her married life and be the mistress of Holden House, her dowry. It was a home she had always loved and couldn't wait to raise their children there.

Brandon had been attentive in the first few weeks of their marriage and then suddenly he was gone all the time. Cecilia was not naïve enough to think he was actually out with his friends. She could smell the stale perfume on him when he arrived home each night, or sometimes in the morning after being gone all night. She tried to bridge the gap that increased between her and her husband, and yet nothing worked. Why didn't he love her the way she loved him? She would swear he was her soulmate—her kindred soul, the one that she had been

1

bound with by the universe since the day she was born. It had become such a contrast to their wedding day and the ache that she felt filled her soul. Her mind drifted back.

The fragrance of the spring air filled the day. The lilacs were in full bloom as Cecilia walked down the aisle towards the gazebo where Brandon stood waiting for her. His smile widened when he saw her and he placed his hand over his heart. Her heartbeat reverberated within her as she walked toward him, her eyes never leaving his. Obvious chemistry grew between them while they courted.

She downed her glass of Scotch. It would infuriate Brandon that she drank his private stash, but she was no longer in a mindset that she cared or that she wanted to please him. He had long given up on keeping his mistress a secret from her. She arrived in town to do some shopping, only to be hit with the fact that his mistress was pregnant. And the hit came as a punch to the gut when she came face to face with her. The shopkeeper had gawked at them as Cecilia tried to stand tall and not shrink back at the sight of her. But the mistress approached Cecilia and demanded that she see what she was up against. The laughter that erupted behind them tore away Cecilia's defenses and she fled with tears racing down her cheeks. She was the talk of the town, her foolish love for her husband who didn't love her and made no qualms about letting everyone know he married her to get the Holden House.

Dragging a chair over to the balcony, she sat for a moment looking down into the foyer. Would he even notice when he walked in the door? How long would it take him to erase every trace of her from the house–the house that should have been their children's home, a home filled with love and laughter?

She grabbed the glass and headed back to the study for another glass of Scotch. She wasn't brave enough to end it all without the liquid courage burning through her. As she made her way down the hall, it hit her how quiet the house was. The servants disappeared shortly after she arrived back home. They could tell she heard the news, and they showed no loyalty to her. They knew who their master was, and she was a nobody. Brandon made that clear to the servants by the way he undermined anything she tried to take control over in the house. He changed the menus she prepared, and it soon became clear that the cook wouldn't even meet with her, as she understood Cecilia had no authority.

She entered the study and glanced around. Everything was in its place. She laughed out loud as the urge to turn everything upside overtook her. She could see his face when he saw it, his fist clenched by his side as rage overtook him. Her laughter slowed to a giggle as the thought of him no longer being able to direct his rage at her made her aware of how bad things really were in their marriage. She loved him, and he resented her. She hated the fact that she was only part of his life so that he could have what he wanted. The grandiose estate was the talk of the town. No expense was spared on the house during construction. It represented an almost majestic quality of the family in residence — well, except for Cecilia. They viewed her as nothing more than a means to the end for the man who held her heart.

She filled her glass again, leaving only a small dreg left in the bottle that she purposefully placed in the middle of his desk. She sipped it as she sank into his desk chair and looked around. Her eyes blurred with unshed tears. She blinked furiously to stop them from flowing.

Downing half the glass, she choked at the burn in the back of her throat.

She rose and grabbed the rope she left on the edge of the desk earlier. This was it. How significant to start their marriage a year ago and end it on their anniversary. He would be so relieved, she was sure, but a small hope rose in her that he would come running through the door, pledging his love, and begging her forgiveness. Would she forgive him? Her heart raced with the hope and she knew that this was a man she would do anything for—anything except continue living in the radiant hate that came from him.

She made her way back up the marble staircase from the foyer to the second floor. The chair sat like a beacon next to the balcony and she walked as if propelled by something greater than herself. Her mind was fuzzy from the Scotch and she took another sip, praying this would be less painful than the past year of living with Brandon.

She tied off the end of the rope to the railing baluster, securing the knot and tugging on it to be sure it would hold. It would do no good if it let go when she went over the edge. She sat in the chair and sipped the Scotch once more. The clock from the study chimed. She counted the chimes. Eleven. It was almost time. She prayed Brandon came through that door soon and found her. Would he feel any sort of remorse or shame for his actions? She doubted it. A man with a heart of stone would feel nothing but relief to be rid of a wife he hated.

Draining the last of the amber liquid, she rose and slid the noose she made around her neck. Pulling her skirt high, she stepped up on the chair and looked down over the balcony. Dizziness washed over her at the height of it.

She grabbed the back of the chair for support and glanced down as the door opened and in stepped Brandon.

She gasped as she realized he was home sooner than she expected. She met his eyes as he glanced up at her. She straightened her shoulders and stared straight into his cold brown eyes. She felt a twinge of hope as he raised his eyebrow at her. That twinge dissipated as she watched him bow to her and smile as he turned, walking back out the door.

The tears coursed unstoppable down her cheeks at that moment. She cried out her love for him as she stepped over the balcony, dropping until the rope broke her neck.

Chapter One

Tara laid still, her eyes adjusting to the darkness. What had woken her up? Was it the recurrent dreams—nightmares—that had her heart racing? The dream was always the same woman talking to her, calling to her, giving her incomprehensible instructions.

She heard the thump again. Slowly, she got out of bed and pulled her robe on, belting it tightly around her waist. She crept to the door and cracked it, listening for some clue to let her know it wasn't her imagination. A creak of the stairway increased the pounding of her heart as she took a step out of the bedroom. She ran her hand along the wall of the hallway, reaching for the light switch at the top of the stairs.

She flipped the switch. Three steps up from the bottom stood a man *inside her house*.

He looked up at her and shock ran across his face. "Who are you?"

"I could ask you the same thing." She wrapped her

arms around her waist to stop the shaking that was starting. Her mind raced to what she could use as a weapon.

"I'm Ryan Stafford. This is my house." He leaned against the railing and waited.

"I rent this place. The owner is off traveling."

Ryan pulled a cell phone from his pocket. "Would you like me to call the police to verify who I am?"

Tara nodded, curious by his calm demeanor. She wanted nothing more than to push him out the door. Yet there was something familiar about his eyes; she couldn't tear herself away from his gaze. The steel blue mesmerized her, but she couldn't think of where she had seen them before. Although startled by his presence, something about him was comforting. She sensed no real danger here with him. *How did she know that?* Her mind tried to grasp for those memories just out of reach. She shook her head with frustration, keeping an eye on him.

Ryan snapped the cell phone shut. His words had registered with her: he was speaking and asking for an officer to come to Stafford House. *Stafford House?* He never stated an address.

"And you think they will know where you are without giving them an address?"

Ryan nodded. "My grandparents were well known in this town. Stafford House is what this homestead has been called since before I was born." He turned and walked down the few stairs he had climbed.

Tara started down the stairs slowly. She hesitated when Ryan glanced up at her.

"They will be here shortly," he said. "Want some coffee?"

Anger hit Tara hard. "Stop. I don't know who you are.

I have *paid* to be here, and I'd prefer you stayed put until the police get here."

Ryan turned to face her. "This is a bit awkward since it's my house, but as you wish." He gave her a mocking bow.

"If this is your house, why didn't you notify me you were coming back?"

Ryan shrugged. "Honestly, I forgot I rented it. I've been traveling for work and had come down quite sick. Once I was okay to travel again, I wanted to return home for a rest."

The story made sense to Tara, but she couldn't shake something was slightly off about everything. His eyes were so familiar, but she didn't know him at all. And that damn nightmare again with the woman telling her to find the boy. *What boy?*

Tara rubbed her temples. A dull headache was starting, and she wanted to curl up in bed and sleep, with no dreams, for a straight eight hours.

A knock at the door startled Tara. She watched as Ryan opened the door. Officer Kelley stepped through the door. "Hi Tara. Heard you had an intruder here tonight?" He flashed a smile at her and she relaxed. Tara relaxed as Officer Kelley spoke. It was a small town and Tara had met him when she arrived, as he had been the one who handled her renting the place. It was one thing she loved about this place: everyone knew everyone. It was the place where people helped other people and Tara had felt that immediately when she came to town and asked about a rental. She had been directed to Bobby, whose friend was out of town and had told Bobby to rent out the place. With payment made for the rental, and a handshake, keys were handed over to her. Tara knew Bobby had run a background check on her and had felt very comfortable with the arrangement. She wasn't locked into a time frame. She was paying monthly as she stayed.

"Do you know this man?"

Officer Kelley turned and stuck out his hand.

Ryan grasped his, and they shook hands. "Good to see you, Bobby."

"Dude, you can't just wander into your house when it's rented out."

The police officer turned towards Tara. "This is the owner of the house. Ryan Stafford. I understand the confusion, but he's actually who he says he is."

Tara nodded. "So what now?"

Officer Kelley turned to Ryan. "You need a place to stay?"

Ryan glanced at Tara. "I've recouped from being quite sick. If it's okay with you, I'll stay in the carriage house?"

"The rental was for the house only, so it's not a problem." Bobby looked up at Tara. "Is that okay with you?"

Tara sighed. She was exhausted and her head was pounding. "Whatever. We'll sort it out in the morning. But just so you know, I have the police department on speed dial in case I need it."

Ryan smiled at her. "Understood."

Tara watched the two men exchange numbers and talk about catching up soon. Tara watched as they both headed towards the door before she turned and started up the stairs. She was about halfway up when she heard the door open.

"Thank you. Good night," Ryan's voice came up the stairs, and she simply nodded before she heard the door close behind them.

After closing her bedroom door, Tara leaned against it. A niggling in the back of her mind teased her, yet she didn't know him from a hole in the ground. She stood for what seemed like an eternity, letting her mind wander, trying to remember what was out of reach. She finally shook her head and crawled back into bed. The thought of the recurrent nightmares forced her to keep her eyes open.

She allowed Ryan's steel-blue eyes to penetrate her thoughts. The Stafford House. She felt she knew that name, yet in the past three months that she had been renting this place, no one had ever called it that. It had always been just the address written. She shivered as she felt herself being pulled into a fitful slumber once again.

Tara ran through the woods. She couldn't see anyone behind her, yet there was an urgency to get away from whatever it was. Her mouth opened to scream, but no sound came out, so she tried to scream louder. Still nothing. She continued running until she suddenly tripped, falling into a deep hole. The dirt gave way beneath her as she tried to climb out of the deep, cavernous gap.

She frantically searched for something to give her a foothold to climb out. A man's voice brought her eyes upward. A hand reached for her, but it was too far out of reach. She tried jumping, and it appeared to get further and further away.

Tara sat upright in bed. Drenched in sweat, her heart raced. The dream she had replayed over and over again every night. Some nights it was her in the hole, but other nights it was her grandmother, who she only knew by voice; but the dream was always the same. She glanced at the clock. Four a.m. She would never go back to sleep now. She got up, pulling on yoga pants and a t-shirt.

Coffee was the only thing that would clear her mind at the moment.

She cautiously made her way downstairs. The house was quiet and dark. She wondered if Ryan was sleeping peacefully and immediately shook her head to clear her mind of such thoughts. Those blue eyes had looked at her like they could see into her soul, and it made her uneasy —not that she felt unsafe, but in a way, she craved to get to know him better and allow him to see the depths of her, including the insecurities, the fear, and the hope for what she believed could be.

She started the coffeemaker and pulled herself up on the counter to sit and wait while it brewed. The aroma assaulted her senses and gave her a feeling of peace as she closed her eyes and inhaled the sweet aroma that had become her lifeline in the long course of sleepless nights and fitful dreams. It was the same routine for her—up early, brew coffee, and then sit and analyze the dreams of the night before while enjoying the morning addiction. She never came up with answers, but she felt a sense of purpose surrounding her dreams.

Tara vaguely remembered her grandmother, her voice anyway. They had talked on the phone, but Tara had no memories of actually seeing her and there had been no pictures in the house of any family members. Tara had no memories before age ten. Everything was a dream, something that could have been, but so far out of reach, it was surreal. The only actual memories she had of her grandmother came from her dreams, and Tara couldn't trust that they were accurate. Her grandmother was always running from something, telling Tara to run or being obscure, telling Tara she needed to "find him." Tara did not know who he was or why she needed to find him.

The coffeemaker beeped, signaling the end of the brewing cycle, and Tara opened her eyes, hearing a slight knock on the back door. She jumped off the counter and opened the door. She looked straight into the steel-blue eyes she had met last night.

"You're awake."

She rolled her eyes. "What do you want?"

"I saw the light on and realized I didn't have any food yet. Can you spare a cup of coffee?"

Tara stepped back and let him in. She went to the cupboard and reached in for two mugs. Ryan nodded and turned towards the fridge. He reached in and grabbed the cream. Tara felt his eyes on her as she poured two mugs full. She doctored hers up with sugar and waited for him to bring the cream over. She glanced over her shoulder as he reached from behind her with the cream. Her eyes met his and held. She caught her breath and held it, not wanting to let the sigh escape her.

"Waiting for this?"

She nodded and willed herself to look away. She let her breath out slowly as he took a step back. She finished fixing her coffee and stepped out of the way for Ryan. She moved backwards, trying not to stare, but the sense of familiarity came over her again and disconcerted her.

"How long have you been gone?" Tara moved to a barstool and slid onto it.

"Ten years, I guess. Give or take. Time all runs together after a while." Ryan turned and leaned against the counter, crossing his ankles.

"What do you do?" Tara sipped her coffee.

"Photography. Travel around, taking pictures and selling them to magazines."

Tara set her mug down. "Doesn't that get old? I mean,

it sounds exciting and all, but ten years is a long time to be gone from home."

Ryan shrugged. "I don't have any family left and too many demons here for me."

Tara's curiosity piqued, but she held her tongue.

"What about you?" Ryan asked. "Why are you hiding out here at Stafford House?"

"Hiding out? Who said I was hiding?" Tara felt a chill grip her.

"Just a figure of speech. Where's your family?"

Tara finished her coffee and spun the mug around and around. "All my family's gone as well." Her voice was small. She hated talking about her family and especially now with all the dreams that kept recurring.

Tara stood abruptly and put her mug in the sink. "I've got things to do. We can talk later about how long you think you are staying and what arrangements I am going to have to make to get out of here."

"It's only five a.m. What could you possibly have to do so urgently at this time of day?" Ryan smirked at her.

"I'm going for a walk." She turned to leave the kitchen.

"Want some company?"

She looked back at him. "I don't know why you would want to go for a walk with me."

"Well, it would give us a chance to get to know each other. I don't think you need to leave. And I think I'd rather take a walk with you than sit here by myself."

She shrugged. "Suit yourself. I'll be leaving in five minutes, whether or not you're ready."

Tara escaped to her room under the guise of getting sneakers, yet she was trembling inside. Her grandmother's voice echoed through her mind. *Find him.* Why now?

Why would her grandmother push her now? Did Ryan have something to do with all this? With what, though? All she knew was she was having nightmares that could be interpreted as her grandmother sending her a message —or she was losing her mind.

Chapter Two

RYAN WAS STANDING ON THE FRONT PORCH WAITING AS TARA came through the door. She had a brief thought that he had changed his mind before seeing him lounging against the railing. She scowled, although inside her stomach clenched in anticipation of spending time with him.

"Thought you might have changed your mind." Tara started down the steps without a glance towards him.

"Not a chance." Ryan fell into step beside her. "So, where're we going?"

Tara glanced up and hesitated a brief second. "I wanted to walk past the old house people claim is haunted."

"Why?" Ryan reached out and grabbed her hand.

Tara stopped. The heat from his hand coursed up her arm, and she instinctively wrapped her fingers around his. "Just morbid curiosity, I guess."

"How long have you been renting the Stafford House?" Ryan started walking again, but continued to hold her hand.

Tara glanced down at their hands. There was a warmth and sense of safety with their hands together, fingers entwined. "About six months. Why?"

"Curiosity. Why this town?"

Tara shook her head. "Are you sure you are a photographer and not an investigative reporter? What's with the interrogation?"

Ryan snickered. "I love a good mystery. Call me an amateur sleuth wannabe."

Tara withdrew her hand, heat flooding her face. "I'm not a mystery. I'm here because I wanted a fresh start. Here seemed just as good as anywhere else." She felt a chill run through her. She was led, she knew, by her grandmother. She wasn't sure why, but there was a reason she was here in this town. But to say that to a stranger would put her fears of being crazy visible for someone else to see.

Ryan wasn't fazed by her response and instead steered her across the street. "Shortcut to the infamous haunted house." He grabbed her hand again to help her through a hole in a fence, but let go before she pulled away.

"What do you know about the house?"

"Old crazy lady used to live here. There's rumors that the family was cursed and everyone died."

Tara stopped short. "How did they die? What curse?" Curiosity coursed through her body and she wondered if it was related to her grandmother's messages.

Ryan turned to look at her. He grinned. "Don't know exactly. Does this stuff freak you out?"

"Kind of, but I'm also fascinated by it."

He chuckled. "Be prepared. I will outrun you if anything comes after us."

"Wow, quite the gentleman." They fell into a comfortable silence and Tara's mind wandered to Ryan's family and childhood. Not sure where the thoughts came from, she allowed herself to enjoy the thought process.

They stumbled over logs and fallen tree branches as they continued down the overgrown path to the house. Tara looked around her and tried to see herself as a child playing in these woods. Familiarity screamed at her, but there were no memories. "Did you come into these woods a lot as a child?"

Ryan glanced back at her. "Yeah. A friend of mine and I used to spend a lot of time running through these parts."

"Still friends?"

Ryan shook his head. "No. I haven't seen her since she was little and moved away. I've been trying to find her, but it's like she fell off the face of the earth."

Tara watched the emotions on Ryan's face. As quickly as they were there, they were gone, and he was back to his joking manner.

"Watch your step. There's a hole up here that's quite deep." Ryan reached out a hand to pull Tara to the left of what looked to be a pile of leaves, but as they moved around it, she saw a gaping hole in the ground. She had a flash before her eyes of a young girl crying for help.

She gasped out loud and shuddered. It took her a minute to realize Ryan had been talking to her. "What?"

"Are you okay? You look like you've seen a ghost." Ryan pulled her closer but kept a small distance between them.

Tara nodded her head. "Of course. I wasn't expecting such a big hole." Truth be told it was the hole from her dream, and she couldn't shake the feeling she had been here before.

"We can go back," Ryan's voice broke through her thoughts. Concern shadowed his face as she glanced up at him.

She shook her head no and gestured for him to continue. A short distance ahead, they broke through a clearing and in front of them stood an abandoned house, looking eerily back at them. Tara shivered and took a step forward. A calmness passed over her, and she closed her eyes. She jumped when a hand rested on her shoulder and she quickly launched herself forward.

Laughter greeted her as she turned to see Ryan bent over in hysterics. Tara shook her head. "Hilarious."

"I couldn't resist. I didn't think you would jump like that." Ryan wrapped his arm around his waist, trying to look sober.

Tara mumbled under her breath, "Happy I can amuse you." She turned back towards the house. "Think we can get in?"

"You don't really want to go in, do you? It probably has rotted floors and isn't safe."

Tara turned to him. "Where's your sense of adventure? Does it stop at scaring me?"

"Is that a challenge?"

Tara laughed. "If it means we go in the house, yeah." She started for the porch, only to have Ryan stop her.

"I think we should come back with a flashlight. It will be dark inside and I would like to see where I'm going."

"The sun's up. There will be light through the windows." Tara tried to take another step, but Ryan stopped her.

"The dirt on the windows won't let the light in. Be reasonable."

Tara sighed. "Fine. Killjoy." She turned to face him. "I think you're scared."

Ryan tucked her hand around his elbow. "My dear, I just want to protect you."

The laughter that erupted from Tara took her by surprise. It had been years since she had laughed like that. The ease and comfort sensation brought out a small part of her that hoped Ryan wouldn't move out of the house so she could get to know him better. They walked in comfortable silence down the street back to the Stafford House. Tara was lost in her thoughts and didn't mind the silence, and could only hope that Ryan felt the same.

Chapter Three

RYAN EXCUSED HIMSELF TO MAKE A FEW PHONE CALLS ONCE they arrived back at the Stafford House. Tara felt a bit relieved, needing to gather her thoughts. She sank down into the glider on the front porch. She smiled to herself thinking of the easy banter between Ryan and herself that morning. Here it was still mid-morning, and she had been up for hours, yet felt so energized. Usually after a sleepless night, she was falling asleep by this time of the day.

In usual fashion, she tried to psychoanalyze her dream. Once again, her mind remained blank as to why she was having recurrent dreams with her grandmother. Her grandmother had been gone for years and she only remembered her from telephone calls and pictures. Tara had never met her personally, that she remembered at least. Her mind wandered from the dreams to her walk in the woods with Ryan. The hole in the ground triggered a vision or a memory of some sort, but she couldn't figure out what it was. It resembled the nightmares she had been having about being trapped in a hole in the ground.

Find him were the words her grandmother kept repeating in the dream and Tara was at a loss as to who *him* was. Why were these dreams happening to her? She had been plagued now for years, almost obsessed, with haunted houses and her research led her to Winchester. On a whim, she rented a house, determined to figure out her fascination with this house. History was scarce as far as who used to live there, but as she got to know people in the town and as they started to trust her, she was finding them opening up a bit.

Maybe it would be a plus to have Ryan here. He may know even more of the history. A small part of her balked at the thought of his staying in a house she was renting, yet she enjoyed his company so much today that her past loneliness was winning out in favor of having him around. She sighed and wished she had more of a family connection. She longed for years for a sister—someone that she could talk things over with. But she had no siblings. And her parents were distraught every time she stated she wished for a sibling.

Tara sighed. Time to put the past behind her and look forward. Maybe focusing on this house wasn't a good idea. It triggered so many childhood memories and things that seemed familiar to her, yet she couldn't quite place it. Like her grandmother. Her mind, having circled back to her grandmother again brought Tara to her feet. It was time to throw herself into something to distract her.

She entered the house to meet Ryan in the foyer as he came downstairs.

"Phone calls all made?"

"For now. I've taken time off from work for the next

month." He paused. "We should probably talk about the house. Do you want me to go?"

Tara searched his face. He looked tired, and his story of being ill and needing to recoup seemed plausible. How could she turn him from his own house? "No. You can stay."

Ryan smiled. "I'll talk to the property management team and they will adjust your rent. No rent while I'm here, and we'll consider you my guest."

"There's no need for that. I can pay my own rent." Tara took a step back. She didn't want to take a handout, although not paying rent would certainly save her some cash.

"I insist. It's the least I can do for allowing me to stay." Ryan shrugged. "Hungry?"

She nodded slowly. "I honestly need more coffee. These sleepless nights are catching up with me."

Ryan watched her quizzically. "You make the coffee. I'll whip up some eggs and toast."

They headed to the kitchen, both silent, their thoughts elsewhere. Tara struggled to maintain a distance and yet there was a pull to Ryan she didn't understand. They busied themselves in the kitchen, keeping silent. Tara was startled when Ryan flipped on the radio. She smiled as she watched him cook, moving in time to the soft country music coming through the speakers.

"If you find this amusing you, wait until you hear me sing."

Tara laughed out loud. "Not a singer, huh?"

"Oh, I could be...I like to save that for the shower." He winked at her as he plated the eggs and toast. "Coffee ready?"

"Yup." She poured two mugs and brought them to the small table in the kitchen's corner. As they sat down to eat, Tara glanced at Ryan and caught him watching her. "Did you poison the eggs?"

"Of course not, just want to make sure you think they are okay before I try them. I'm not much of a cook."

She shook her head and took a bite. "Delish." She got the one word out as she continued to shovel food into her mouth, not realizing how hungry she had been until she tasted the eggs. She took a breather when she finished her eggs to reach for her toast and realized Ryan sat there watching her.

"Have you never seen a girl eat before?"

"Of course I have, but usually they nibble daintily, not eat like a football player." He ate his eggs one small bite at a time as how he imagined she should have been eating.

Tara scoffed. "Food gets cold that way."

Ryan grinned as he inhaled the rest of his food. "You must have had brothers the way you eat."

Tara sat back in her chair, picking up her coffee. She took a sip. "Nope, no siblings." She stood suddenly and took her plate to the sink. "Just leave the dishes and I will wash them later. I'm going to finish my coffee on the porch. Thanks for breakfast."

She escaped the room. Anxiety filled her chest when he mentioned siblings. Anxiety was something she had dealt with for years. It was always unknown, yet centered on her family or the thought of a bigger family that she never had. Over the years, she became accustomed to walking away from any situation that made her chest ache to the point of being painful. She shook her head and tried to clear the thoughts from her mind. As she eased into a chair on the porch, she closed her eyes and inhaled deeply, and exhaled, trying to push the pain from her chest.

The chest tightness subsided with each breath she drew and she finally opened her eyes. Ryan sat on the railing, watching her. "You okay?"

"What are you doing?"

Ryan stood and sat in the chair next to her. "I was worried the way you bolted from the room. What happened?"

Tara shook her head. She concentrated on taking a few sips of coffee before she would meet his eyes. "It's nothing."

Ryan sat back and put his legs up on the railing. Silence fell between them. Tara felt like a fool for not saying anything. But she saw her anxiety as a weakness and she didn't want questions asked. She finished her coffee. She leaned her head back and closed her eyes. She felt comforted by the fact that Ryan was next to her and yet she felt awkward, like she should say something. Her answer to the awkwardness, of course, was to close her eyes and try to forget he was there.

She opened one eye at the sound of Ryan's phone going off. He quickly answered it and rose silently in an attempt to not disturb her. She closed her eyes again and relaxed as she heard the front door shut behind him. She drifted off to sleep as a calmness washed over her.

She was a child again, running through the woods as her laughter filled the surrounding air. She heard him behind her, telling her she was cheating again. He was such a poor sport sometimes, yet the competition between them was strong and it drove her to beat him every chance she could. She ducked under a branch. He called out that he twisted his ankle and she turned to look, only to have him pass her, laughing. She

25

pushed herself to run faster. The ground gave way, and she found herself in a hole. She screamed for him. There was no way out. She tried climbing, but the dirt gave way and she fell back down into the hole. She could hear him calling her name and see his arm reaching towards her, but it was out of reach.

Tara jumped a mile when the door slammed shut. She opened her eyes and saw the porch and Ryan standing at the top of the stairs.

"Everything okay?" She shook her head to clear the cobwebs from her mind.

"Yeah, work stuff. I didn't realize you had fallen asleep. Sorry to wake you."

Tara brushed his apology aside. "No worries. I shouldn't be sleeping at this time of day, anyway."

"You're exhausted, though. Are you not sleeping at all at night?" The concern in his voice startled Tara as she looked up at him.

"No, not really." She sighed. It had become the norm for her.

"What's going on? Anything I can help with?" Ryan sat down in the chair he had been in earlier, resuming the previous pose with his legs sprawled out in front of him on the railing.

"No. Just a recurrent nightmare that I can't seem to place. I..." She allowed her voice to trail off. She couldn't tell him that the hole at the haunted house was the same one in her dream. He would think she was nuts. Hell, she thought she was nuts herself.

"Maybe if you talk it through."

Tara shook her head and stood. "I'm fine. I need to run to the store and get some things. Anything you need?"

"Nope, I'm good." Ryan closed his eyes. Tara mentally

breathed a sigh of relief. She had feared he would want to go with her. At least she had an excuse to get out of the house and away from the unsettling things running through her mind. Fear and uncertainty–two very powerful motivators to do the wrong thing.

Chapter Four

TARA HAD ESCAPED THE INSANITY ONCE AGAIN. SHE INHALED A deep breath and slowly exhaled. She needed space from Ryan. He gave the impression of enjoying her company... or did he? Why did he ask so many questions about her family? Her racing heart slowed as she walked down the sidewalk.

She had a flashlight on her phone and she was determined to get into the so-called haunted house before the day was done. There was something about it, calling to her. Her grandmother's voice kept telling her to break the curse and find the boy. Recurrent headaches had started flaring every time she tried to remember her childhood. There were no memories of home, her family. She could hear her grandmother's voice, but couldn't put a face to the voice. There was no memory of her attending school before she was ten. Why not?

Her parents couldn't provide those answers now that they were gone. The tragic car accident that took both of them away from her always tore through Tara's heart whenever she thought of them. It was unnecessary. They had gone to the store and a truck without brakes blew through the stop sign, killing them both instantly. She was alone now. No family, no memories and nothing but a crazed ghost of her grandmother giving her insane directions. Tara had thought on more than one occasion that she should see a shrink, but couldn't give up on the thought that she still had a connection with her grandmother and wanted to keep that to herself before she lost the last connection she had to her family.

Tears filled her eyes, and she blinked fast to clear them. She stopped and in front of her stood the grand old house. It was weather-beaten from sitting empty so long without the upkeep. The paint was chipping off and grime covered the windows. She trudged up the walkway, glancing around and seeing no one. She slipped around to the back of the house. The back veranda was warped and signs of rotting in the wood were obvious. She took one cautious step forward and then another, being careful to avoid the rotted areas.

She felt a warm breeze blow by her as she turned the handle to the back door. It opened with no problems. She pushed it opened and stood outside the threshold. Tara closed her eyes, taking a deep breath. The warm breeze pushed against her and she opened her eyes as she stepped inside.

Find him, the voice resonated inside her.

"Gram, are you here?" Tara's voice shook as she called out, knowing it was impossible.

Find him.

Tara shook her head as if she could clear the voice. Her grandmother had become a nuisance lately with that phrase. "Who?"

The silence was deafening, and Tara took another

step into the house. She had entered the kitchen. Dust covered everything. Dishes were still in the dish drain beside the sink. Tara wandered over to the sink and ran her fingers lightly over the dishes. She closed her eyes and left her hand still, willing herself to feel something... anything.

"What are you doing here by yourself?" The male voice behind her made Tara jump a mile, turning around sheepishly.

Ryan leaned against the doorframe. "I needed to see the inside."

"Why? Don't you know it's not safe for you to come in here alone?"

"Why do you care what I do?" Tara took a defensive stance, her arms crossed across her chest. "I'm not your concern."

"Well, since we kind of share a house these days, maybe I feel protective."

"You're not even supposed to be here. Don't interfere with my life." Tara stormed out of the house and onto the back porch. She picked her way around the rotten boards and stopped once she was back on the ground. She felt his presence beside her before he even spoke.

"I'm not trying to interfere. I want you safe." His voice was soft, and Tara turned to face him. There was real concern shining from those steel-blue eyes and Tara felt a stab of guilt.

"I'm sorry. It probably wasn't smart for me to go in alone. I just...wanted to be by myself." Tara started to take a step away, but turned suddenly back towards Ryan. "How did you even know I was here?"

"A hunch. You were gone longer than I figured you would be if you went to the grocery store. You wanted to get in here this morning." Ryan shrugged. "But if you didn't mind me being here this morning, why sneak back here without me now?"

"I don't know." Tara played with her cell phone. "I couldn't get it out of my mind."

"Well, let's do it then. I'll give you space, but I think we should go in together. There is rotten wood and if you get hurt and I'm not here, I could never forgive myself."

Tara nodded. "Okay."

Ryan stepped back to allow her to pass. Tara made her way up the porch steps again and across to the back door. Stepping into the kitchen, she was oddly aware that there was no warm breeze this time pushing against her. She sighed. Would her grandmother not show up if Ryan was here?

Tara moved beyond the kitchen this time. She stepped into the hallway that led to the front of the house. Moving slowly, she took in the pictures hanging on the wall. She stopped suddenly when a picture caught her eye. It was filthy and hard to see the people with all the grime on the glass. She took it off the wall and wiped her hand across it. Instead of clearing it, she smudged the dirt, making the picture even less visible.

Ryan reappeared beside her and held out a towel. Tara took it and continued to clean it until she could see the picture. She opened the flashlight app on her cell phone and shined it on the picture. It couldn't be!

"Who used to live here?" She demanded.

"Just some crazy lady. She kept to herself. The town thought she was a witch or something. There was some story of a curse to her family."

The warm breeze blew against Tara and she dropped the picture. The glass broke as it hit the floor.

"Did you feel that?"

"Feel what?" Ryan stared at her. "Are you okay?"

Tara nodded. She turned towards the living room. The furniture was covered with cloths. She moved into the middle of the room and turn around slowly, taking in every corner. There was something so familiar about it, but she couldn't pinpoint it.

"Gram?" she whispered.

I must be going insane. Tara stopped moving and closed her eyes. She had been here before, she knew it. The warm breeze enveloped her. She wrapped her arms around her body and relaxed at the sensation of being hugged. "Gram, please talk to me."

"Tara?" Ryan's voice broke her concentration. She felt the warm breeze lift from around her and her frustration grew. "You okay?"

She nodded and moved towards the foyer and the stairs to the second floor. "You going to follow me up here, too?"

Ryan's face registered shock. "What's with the snippiness?"

A picture dropped from the wall to the floor, glass breaking. Tara's glance darted to the picture that had fallen. It was two young children. She hurried the few steps to pick up the picture from the mess on the floor. The little girl was hanging onto the boy's hand and smiling. She peered closely at it. Steel-blue eyes looked back at her from the picture.

Turning towards Ryan, she held out the picture. "Do you know these kids?"

Ryan took the picture and started smiling. "That's me and Anna."

"Anna?"

He nodded. "She was my best friend. We did everything together. Her parents moved when we were six. I haven't seen or talked to her since. Wow, this brings back memories."

"Did you know the lady that lived here?"

"As I remember, it was some relative of Anna's. Her parents never said much, but I remember being here a few times. She gave us cookies she had made. My parents told me I could play with Anna, but I wasn't supposed to come here to the house."

"Why?" Tara took the picture back and looked at it. The tilt of the girl's head sparked a memory of other pictures she had seen once while she was snooping in the attic when she was a teenager.

"I don't remember. Everyone in town thought she was a witch and was afraid of her. I remember her as being gentle and kind the few times I saw her. Anna loved her." Ryan kicked at the glass on the floor. "I wonder whatever happened to Anna."

"You should search for her on social media. Most everyone is on it in some form these days." Tara handed the picture back to him. "Do you want to keep this?"

Ryan nodded. Taking the picture from Tara, he moved out of the way as she headed for the stairs again.

"Come on." She shrugged as she crept up the stairs, testing each one before putting her full weight on it. Tara reached the top of the stairs and instinctively turned towards the right. There was a door at the end of the hall and another was about halfway down on the left side of the hall. She took a few steps and stopped. Ryan had started in the other direction.

"Aren't you coming with me?"

"I thought you wanted your space?"

Tara bit her bottom lip as uneasiness flooded her. "Maybe we should stick together."

Ryan nodded and walked over to her. He took her hand and waited for her to proceed. She squeezed his hand and started forward. There was something comforting in the warmth of Ryan's hand in hers. She stopped in front of the door to the left of the hallway. Ryan reached in front of her and opened the door, pushing it open slowly.

A bathroom. Wallpaper was peeling off the walls. Tara glanced in and gestured toward the other door at the end of the hallway. They moved slowly, in time together, stopping in front of the door. Again, Ryan pushed it open and waited.

Tara realized she was holding her breath when she exhaled at the sight of the room. It had a canopy bed and a dollhouse in the corner. Tara immediately was drawn to the dollhouse. She squatted in front of it and placed her hand on top of it. She closed her eyes and a flash of a child playing in this very spot popped into her mind. Just as quick, it was gone.

Find him. Let him save you, her grandmother's voice whispered in her ear. Tara trembled. What? Who was this child that kept flashing into her mind? Could it be Ryan's friend, Anna?

"Tara, what is it?"

Tara stood up, still trembling. "I don't know. I keep getting these flashes. Like a memory, but I don't think it's mine." She sighed. "I know it sounds insane."

Ryan pulled her closed to him and wrapped his arms tight around her, holding her until the shivering stopped. "Not insane. Some people are more in tuned to others, spirits, things like that."

Tara nodded against his chest.

"Do you want to talk about them?"

"Not now. Let's go. I'm suddenly exhausted." She pulled away, and the warmth was gone. She ached to feel those powerful arms around her again. He brought a peace to her, and she didn't understand why.

They were silent as they walked back to Stafford House. Tara struggled with trying to piece it all together, and the harder she tried to bring back the visions, the more it eluded her. Even her grandmother's voice had gone silent for the time being. Ryan hadn't let go of her hand since they left the haunted house...haunted. Was it really haunted or was that the story that attached itself to the house through years of rumors around town?

There was still so much to learn of this town and that house...thinking about it exhausted Tara.

Chapter Five

RYAN'S MIND SPUN OUT OF CONTROL. THE PICTURE OF ANNA and him as children was in his back pocket of his jeans. Tara had picked up the picture of the couple that she had first held when they arrived at the house. He had no idea who they were—hadn't gotten a good look at the picture. Something had changed in Tara's demeanor; a fear had overtaken her and he was almost afraid to talk about it with her.

His mind drifted to when he was a child and the hours he spent running these woods with Anna until that awful day she fell into the hole. He had refused to leave her to go get help, terrified she would disappear if he left. He struggled for what seemed like hours to reach her and finally had pulled her out of the hole.

Her parents had packed up and left the next day. It was the last memory he had with her, and it was a terrifying one. One that haunted him for years as a child. He had contacts now through his work. Maybe he could find Anna and at least see where she was in life and how she was doing. The old woman from the haunted house had died a few years ago and Ryan had missed the funeral as he was out of town for work. He had heard that no one showed up for it and that the minister said a small prayer before she was buried in an unmarked grave behind her house.

Rumor was the house had been left to her granddaughter, who hadn't been located after all these years. Was Anna her granddaughter? If she was, how did he think he could find her when the lawyers weren't able to?

He wanted to comfort Tara, but as they continued on in silence, he had no idea what to say. She appeared overwhelmed. He had hated it when she had stepped out of his arms back at the house. He wanted to hold her, kiss away her tears, and assure her they would solve whatever it was that was troubling her together.

Ryan ran through options in his mind. He could hire a private investigator to look for Anna, but in his gut, he knew that would be a dead end. It was like she had fallen off the face of the earth. He could trace back the ancestry of Anna's family and see what he could find, maybe a clue to who actually owned the house for all these years and the history.

Being a photographer, a mystery always fascinated him, and old pictures in the house were the place to start. He planned on getting back to the house and checking out the rest of the photographs without Tara. He didn't want to upset her.

He allowed himself to remember those childhood times that he had tried so hard to forget all these years. He had been heartbroken when Anna left. Even as a young child, he had a strong connection with her he had never, ever again felt with anyone else. They had been kindred souls, and he still had an empty hole where she used to be.

Once they reached the Stafford House, Tara said she needed to lie down and went on to her bedroom. Ryan was left to his own devices. He paced around the living room with the picture of him and Anna in his hands. He would stop and stare at it every so often before resuming his pacing. Not being able to take it anymore, he grabbed his cell phone and punched in a number.

"Jake, I need a favor."

"Hey, man. Where are you? It's been quite a while since we've spoken."

Jake was an older friend from childhood, the only one that knew about Anna, and had since gone into the PI business. "I'm good. Got sick from my last bout of travels and have ended up back home. Long story, but I need you to do some digging for me."

"On?"

"Remember Anna? I need to find her."

The silence was deafening as Ryan waited for Jake to respond. "Yeah, I remember. Weird shit happened when she was around. Why do you want to find her?"

"I need to. It's a long story, and one I can't go into right now. Can you help?"

Ryan heard the sigh through the phone and knew his friend wouldn't say no to him. "I guess. I'll see what I can find."

"Thanks, man. We'll talk soon."

"Right." The line went dead, and Ryan resumed his pacing.

Tara was sleeping. He could go back to the house and get the pictures. A twinge of guilt hit him, knowing that she had some connection with the pictures. He had seen it in her face. Fear and recognition followed by uncertainty had passed over her. He couldn't do it. He couldn't go behind her back. They were going to have to work together on this and find the story behind that house and what happened to Anna... and how Tara was connected to it all.

Ryan wandered into the kitchen and started brewing some coffee. There was no way to relax his mind enough to get some sleep. Although it was only early afternoon, it felt like he had been up for hours. He stared at the picture of Anna and him, smiling like there were no cares in the world. He remembered this picture being taken. The lady in the house had given them cookies and taken the picture right before they left. It had been the day before Anna had fallen in the hole. The day that changed everything.

Her parents had packed up, and in a flurry, they were gone. He watched them disappear down the road and had stood there for an hour afterwards, willing them to bring her back to him. He had been ten and remembered vividly the ache in his heart as they drove out of sight. He had written to her and taken the letters to the lady at the house, begging her to mail them to Anna. The lady had taken every one of them and promised she would send them to her. He never heard back from Anna.

Shortly after that, the rumor around town was that the lady was crazy talking about curses and her family was all dead because of the curse. Ryan had been told to stay away from the house that soon became labeled as the haunted house in town and everyone shunned the lady that lived there. He couldn't even remember her name.

The coffee maker beeped, indicating the brewing

cycle being done, drawing Ryan from his memories. He poured a cup and was doctoring it up when he heard the voice. *Help her*. He turned and saw no one. He couldn't place the voice, but he had heard it before. Where? Who was it? Help who?

He sipped his coffee, trying to shut his mind off. He couldn't take it anymore. The thoughts of Anna had brought back a pain that ripped his heart in two. He needed her back in his life.

"Did you make enough for me?" Tara whispered from the door.

He nodded and reached for another mug. He fixed her a cup and turned to hand it to her to find her at his side. "Couldn't rest?"

She shook her head. "It's weird. The dreams are coming now and I'm not sleeping. They are like memories, but I don't think they are my memories. Is that possible?"

Ryan reached for her hand. He had to touch her, comfort her. Lacing his fingers with hers, he pulled her closer to him. He looked down into her eyes and froze. The eyes. They looked right into his soul. "I think anything is possible in this crazy world."

His heart raced as she leaned into him. They stood motionless, each lost in their own thoughts. Ryan tried to focus on anything but the way her hair smelled like strawberries and the warmth that he found comforting, even though he wanted to comfort her. He inhaled and slipped their hands entwined together behind her back, pulling her closer. They both held coffee mugs in their free hands, seemingly lost in the moment.

He glanced down. Tara's eyes were closed. He kissed her gently on the forehead, his lips lingering against her skin. Her soft sigh registered with him as she stepped back a step, keeping her hand tightly in his.

"There's so many unanswered questions."

"Let's talk out your dreams and see if we can figure them out? It's got to be better than us fighting our memories and having no answers."

She nodded. "I don't know how to explain them. They are so disjointed. Vaguely familiar, yet I have no recollection of it."

"What do you mean?"

"I see these eyes. They look so familiar, and yet I can't place them to anyone I know." She met his gaze. His steel-blue eyes, full of concern, never left her. Those steel-blue eyes. Where had she seen them before? They weren't in her dream. She saw no faces in her dreams.

"What eyes?"

She shook her head. "I don't know. I don't know where I have seen them. I don't see faces in the dreams." She sipped her coffee. "It's a child in the dream, running and falling. Then a hand reached for the child." She trembled. It was so real.

"Child? How old?" The sharpness of Ryan's voice sounded foreign even to his own ears.

"I don't know. I can't see her clearly. I think it's a girl." Tara finished her coffee, disengaging her hand from Ryan's, and went to the sink to rinse the mug. "I don't know."

Ryan ran his fingers through his hair. Frustration built up in him and he wanted to scream. He knew Tara was trying, but he needed more. The overwhelming urge to fix this and make things whole for her again shook him to the core.

"Tara, have you ever been to this town before?"

"Not that I know of. I don't remember it."

"What brought you here?"

Tara turned and faced him. "My grandmother."

Ryan cocked his head at her, puzzled. "I thought she was dead."

"You're going to think I'm crazy."

"No, I'm not. Talk to me."

"She is dead. I hear her voice, feel her. She didn't come right out and tell me to come here, but this town kept pulling me here. I think she guided me here." Tara shrugged her shoulders.

"And what brought you to Stafford House?" Ryan leaned against the counter, his mind reeled in the possibilities of a mystery. His favorite pastime...chasing down leads for a good story.

"I don't know. It was for rent, and so I rented it. There was no reason. There wasn't anything else at the time for rent." Tara's voice showed her uncertainty.

"Come on. Let's try something." Ryan grabbed her hand and led her to the living room. He gestured for her to sit on the couch. Sitting across from her in a chair, he leaned forward, elbows on knees. "Close your eyes."

"For what?" Tara sat stiffly.

"Relax and close your eyes. Trust me, please." Ryan softened his voice, hoping his calmness would calm her.

She leaned back and closed her eyes. Her hands were clenched into fists at her side. He crossed and sat next to her. He placed his left hand over her right one, moving his thumb in circles on her fist until her hand relaxed.

"Keep your eyes closed. Relax your mind as much as possible and let your mind take you to the first memory of your childhood."

Tara sighed. "I was happy. My parents and me. We

saw my grandmother a lot, but I can't see her face anymore. I haven't for years, even though we talked regularly on the phone after we moved."

"Moved? Where did you move to?" Ryan softly interjected.

"I don't know. I don't remember where we were before. I lost my best friend when we moved. I remember crying for days because we couldn't talk…" Tara's eyes flew open. She clenched at Ryan's hand. "I never remember that… who was my best friend? Why did I lose them?"

"I don't know, but we'll find out." Ryan pulled her into his arms. "We'll do this slow and maybe the memories will come back."

Ryan sat, his hand sliding up and down Tara's arm. The tension left her and she relaxed against him. He continued to hold her, lost in his thoughts. "Have you been to the library and researched the haunted house?"

She shook her head no against his chest.

"Well, that's where we start then. Let's find out who owned the house and maybe that will trigger some more memories for you." Ryan held her close. "What's the earliest memory you consciously remember as a child?"

"I don't have any memories before being ten. It's like there are no memories. I didn't exist."

"What about pictures?"

Tara pulled back and looked up at Ryan. "I have no pictures of me as a child. Even growing up, there were no baby pictures or of me as a young child."

"Who was in the picture you took from the house today?"

"I don't know. For a moment, I thought it was my

parents, but it's so grimy it's hard to tell." Tara laid her head back on Ryan's chest. "I'm afraid to look at it."

Ryan's phone rang. He reluctantly disengaged himself from Tara and reached for the phone, seeing Jake's number flashing. "Yeah?"

"Am I interrupting?" Jake's laughter came across the phone, rubbing Ryan the wrong way.

"Of course not. What's up?"

"We need to talk, man. I'm coming to town. I'll be there tomorrow." Jake didn't wait for a response and the phone was dead before Ryan could respond.

Chapter Six

TARA SPENT ANOTHER RESTLESS NIGHT, DREAM FILLED, THAT SHE could not shake. As much as she would wake herself up and doze back off, the dreams continued in the same spot. Fear gripped her, making it hard to breathe. More than once through the night, Tara woke up gasping for air, feeling a tightening around her throat as if she was being choked to death. The sensation of fingers wrapped around her neck continued even when she was awake.

Her grandmother's voice was faint but continued the mantra of *find him and break the curse*. Tara finally sat up in bed, holding her head in her hands, and wept. Tears soaked her blanket as it caught the river that flowed from her eyes. She was lost and alone. At this point, all she wanted was to die and be done with all these nightmares, memories of someone else, and the fear that clenched at her.

A soft knock at her door brought her head up. She listened, thinking she had imagined it. Another soft knock with Ryan's voice, "Tara?"

"Come in."

The door opened and Ryan slipped in. "Are you okay?"

"Yeah. Can't sleep."

Ryan slipped onto the bed beside her and pulled her close. He laid back on her pillow, cradling her in his arms and held her. "Another dream?"

"I can't stop them. I feel like I'm dying and it's all I can do to wake up." Tara snuggled closer. "Why is this happening to me?"

"I don't know." Ryan placed a soft kiss on her forehead. "See if you can rest with me here."

They laid in silence, and soon Tara's breathing evened out and became deep, indicating her sleeping. Ryan tightened his arms around her, willing his strength to go through to her. A warm air brushed over him. Tara's body relaxed further, stretching out against his, her leg extending over his. His body responded, and he closed his eyes. Trying to think of anything but Tara and the warmth she brought to him, he willed his body to relax and not respond to her. He couldn't complicate things, but God he wanted her. He never had felt such a stirring for someone, a deep connection with anyone. No one except for Anna when they were kids.

Anna...his kindred soul...his lost love and best friend. She had left a hole in him he had tried to fill. When he lost his parents, he ran from everything, taking the traveling photography job that led him on adventures that he never thought would be possible; more than once he had dreamed that Anna was with him sharing all the fun and excitement.

He drifted off to sleep with memories of Anna filling his mind and yet Tara's face becoming more and more present in his dreams. They blended into one person and his heart tore in two. Anna's face faded as the car faded from his memory and he called and called to her. Yet it was Tara's face that kept popping up. Tara's face staring at him from the hole in the ground, Tara's face fading with the car disappearing. He couldn't distinguish them and he cried out.

"Ryan?"

He opened his eyes. Tara was leaning over him, her hand on his cheek. "I'm okay."

"Nightmare for you too?"

"I guess. I can't remember what it was now." He tightened his arms around her. He wanted nothing more than to pull her close and kiss those soft pink lips that were hovering so close to his.

Her tongue ran across her bottom lip before she bit down gently on it. Her eyes were searching his. He ran his hand up her back to her neck. She nodded and brought her lips down to his. He angled her to open her more fully to him. Her tongue stroked his as a soft moan escaped her. He became demanding and pulled her closer, turning to be on his side facing her. She rolled back, bringing him half on top of her.

Ryan broke off the kiss, staring down at her. "Are you sure?"

"I want you, Ryan. I need to feel something other than fear."

Her tentative reply, although the right words, her voice was filled with uncertainty and Ryan pulled back. "Not now, not like this." He kissed her soft and put a bit more space between them. "We need to get some answers before we allow this to get more complicated."

A lone tear escaped Tara's eye and ran down into her hairline. Ryan ran his thumb across her temple to erase it. "Don't. Please don't cry."

"I'm so overwhelmed. I don't know what I'm supposed to be feeling, doing. I feel like I don't even know who I am anymore."

Ryan held her close. Her shoulders tensed against his arms and she was rigid. "Tara, just relax."

She pushed against him. "I can't. I'm going to make coffee."

He sat up and watched her slip into some yoga pants and pull a sweatshirt over her tank top. "You can't keep making coffee in the middle of the night to avoid sleeping."

"Do you want some?"

With a sigh, he nodded and climbed out of bed. "Let's get coffee." He needed answers. He turned towards his room and called to her as she started down the stairs. "I'm going to grab my laptop. I'll be right down."

This needed to stop and he was determined to find answers.

Ryan settled at the kitchen table while Tara paced the kitchen waiting for the coffee to brew. He opened his laptop and pulled up Google. As he punched in *Holden House*, an icy chill settled around him. Not much came up for search results. There was an article talking about the house and the folklore of it being cursed.

"There is nothing online except speculation on the curse of the Holden House on a ghost hunting site."

Tara set a cup of coffee in front of him. "Okay. So, what now?"

"We try town records in the morning...well, at a decent hour this morning." He sat back in his chair and watched Tara play with her coffee. She wasn't really drinking it, and agitation rolled off her.

"We need to find out your family history, Tara. You

said you had no recollection of any family beyond your parents and your grandmother."

She nodded.

"What was your grandmother's name?"

Tara closed her eyes and shook her head. "Grandma? I have no recollection of anything. Why is that?" Tears threatened to spill over her lashes and she blinked hard.

Ryan sighed. "I don't know. What about that picture you took from the house?"

"I would swear they were my parents, but much younger of course. I don't know. There were never any photographs when I was growing up of any family, or myself, before the age of ten." She stood and resumed her pacing. "This is ridiculous. It's like I had no life before that age and then poof I was just here. How is that possible?"

"I don't know." The coffee Ryan had consumed sat like a rock in his stomach. Every sense he had was tingling with apprehension. Something was wrong, very wrong in this scenario and he only hoped Jake could come up with some answers. "My friend, Jake, will be here later today. Maybe he can help us out."

"How can he help?"

"He's a PI and has lots of contacts to dig for information. Let's talk to him and see what he can do."

Tara nodded. "I think I'll go for a run." She was out of the room before Ryan could reply. He stared after her. She was an enigma, but the chill he felt prior was gone. Did he really believe in ghosts?

Chapter Seven

TARA HAD CHANGED QUICKLY INTO HER RUNNING CLOTHES. SHE stepped out onto the porch to put her sneakers on, praying Ryan didn't follow her. She stretched before starting at a slow jog down the sidewalk in the opposite direction of the Holden House. Her mind filled with questions and yet, Ryan kept popping into her mind. His blue eyes kept bringing back the nightmare of the young girl in the hole.

She increased her speed. She needed to outrun these memories of some unknown person who kept popping into her mind. She gasped for air as she came to a stop. She had pushed herself beyond her typical limits and with a stitch in her side, she bent over trying to catch her breath. A warm breeze enveloped her and she sighed. Gram. She had come to know that warm breeze was what she perceived as her grandmother. It was the cold air when it hit her that made her think of death and panic would ensue.

The warm breeze stayed close to her, caressing her arms and relaxing her. Her mind cleared for a moment before her parents' faces appeared in her memory. They were younger and Tara sensed there was more to the memories that she was suddenly being flooded with. She walked towards the park and sat down in a swing.

As she swung back and forth gently, she closed her eyes and tried to remember her childhood. There were no memories before age ten. She remembered a tiny apartment that they lived in. Her mother had homeschooled her and she had never been allowed to go anywhere by herself. It had become more challenging as she grew older and longed for a bit of freedom. Her mother had pushed and pushed to keep Tara from everyone, until Tara threatened to run and go live with her grandmother. Her grandmother. Her grandmother was really just a voice on the phone.

Tara had no memory of what her grandmother looked like. She had called Tara weekly and talked to her, encouraging her to stay close to her parents, but the lack of pictures in Tara's home suddenly angered her. Why? What had her parents been involved in that they shut her away from everyone and everything?

No explanation came to her and she stood and turned towards the Stafford House. She jogged slowly back, hoping that Ryan would have gone back to bed so she wouldn't have to see him. She had been ready to give him what he wanted, but she wasn't looking for a relationship. She wanted the sex, the escape from reality for a little bit. She was attracted to Ryan, and felt a connection, but there was something that just was nagging at her that wasn't quite right.

Those eyes haunted her. Someone with similar eyes from her past had haunted her for years. And after seeing him with the picture of his friend, Anna, she knew where his heart really was. Anna held his heart and probably always would. Tara wouldn't put herself in that position of being second fiddle to anyone, whether it be a real person or a ghost.

She slowed to a walk as she approached the Stafford House. The warm breeze left her and she felt a chill replace the warmth she had experienced. She shivered as she ran up the stairs and into the house. Once inside she instantly warmed, but it wasn't the same as having her Gram wrapped around her.

"Oh, Gram. I need you now more than ever." Tara started upstairs for a shower. She heard voices coming from the kitchen and stopped on the third stair to listen. She couldn't make out the words, but it sounded like Ryan was angry. She jogged up the rest of the stairs and headed for the shower. She couldn't face him right now, not after the way she had lusted after him. Maybe a cold shower would be appropriate.

She stripped down and stepped into the lukewarm water. Tara closed her eyes and allowed the water to rain down on her. She stood with her hand against the wall of the shower, willing the water to wash away the fear and anxiety she felt. She opened her eyes as the water turned cold. She shivered and cranked the handle to hot. The water continued to run cold. She lathered up and rinsed as quick as she could before shutting off the water.

Drying off, she dressed quickly. Pulling a sweatshirt over her head, she called down to Ryan. "What's up with no hot water?"

She heard the water running in the kitchen. "There's hot water," he yelled back.

"Not in the shower." She started down the stairs in

her bare feet and stopped halfway down as Ryan stepped into the foyer from the kitchen.

"There's hot water. Are you sure you had it on hot?" He grinned at her.

"I'm sure. I cranked it as hot as it could go and it was freezing." Shrugging, she finished her descent and went to the living room. She curled up in the corner of the couch and pulled a blanket over her legs. "I'm still cold."

"Are you coming down with something?"

She shook her head. "I'm so tired of feeling like I'm being pulled in multiple directions. Feeling hot and then cold." Tara laid her head against the back of the couch and closed her eyes. She was exhausted. She found sleep when the warm breeze enveloped her again. With a sigh, she allowed her grandmother to hold her and keep her safe.

———

Ryan saw the moment she relaxed. As he had been observing her the past couple of days, he could tell when she had moments of relaxation. Her face would soften. The dark circles under her eyes screamed from her lack of sleep and his stomach clenched in apprehension of the unknown of what was going on. Every time Tara relaxed, it was suddenly warm near her. Did he really believe in spirits and the energy they brought with them?

He had questioned his friend, Jake, about them, asking him to dig up as much information as he could regarding spirits. Jake had joked, but Ryan knew Jake was a big believer in the afterlife. He expected Jake to arrive today, in a few hours, and he stood as Tara slept and left her to rest in peace.

Peace. Not something he had experienced since Tara had arrived in his life. Well, actually since he had crashed her rental and threw himself into her life. He didn't know what the attraction was—yes, there was physical attraction, but it was more than that. His soul ached for her just has he had as a child for Anna.

There was an opposing force at the Holden House that caught him off guard when they had been there. It had been frightening, not so much that he feared for himself, but he had feared greatly for Tara. Nothing he could pinpoint, but there was an evilness there that he couldn't explain. It was a warmer feeling here at the Stafford House when they were together. Fear didn't grip him here at home. Maybe, just maybe he could get a little sleep himself before Jake arrived.

Chapter Eight

JAKE DROVE UP IN FRONT OF THE DILAPIDATED HOUSE. THE house that as children had been the talk of the town. He had never spent time here like Ryan and Anna had, but there was always trouble that surrounded it. Anna had been constantly hurt whenever they ventured near the house.

Jake remembered the final straw. The day Anna had fallen into the hole. Ryan had refused to leave her side and unknown to anyone else, he had somehow saved her. Old Lady Holden said it was pure love that saved her. They were gone within a couple of days. Anna's parents had packed them up and disappeared. He had stayed by Ryan's side as he cried for the loss of his best friend. Jake, to this day, has never seen anyone so heartbroken.

He had his reservations about trying to find Anna for Ryan. Yes, he had the resources and the means to probably track her down, but all these years Ryan didn't need that kind of heartache again. Jake vowed years ago to protect his best friend from that intense hurt at all costs.

Jake stared at the Holden House. He blinked hard,

trying to clear his vision. The curtain -- did it just move in that front room? He shook his head. Impossible. Yet, he put the car in gear and headed toward Stafford House. The quicker he could help Ryan get this solved, the quicker he could make escape from this town once again.

————

Tara sat quietly in the waiting room of the Reiki Master she had found. Reiki relaxed her and ground her from the stress that tended to press on her. She was long overdue for a session and lately with the sleepless nights, she needed something to get her feet back on the ground and out of the nightmares that were consuming her.

"Tara, welcome."

"Hi." Tara stood and approached the young woman standing at the door of the calming room.

"I'm Paula. What are you looking to achieve today?"

Tara stepped into the room, glancing around. "I need to alleviate some stress. I haven't been sleeping well, a lot of nightmares."

Paula nodded and gestured to the table. "You mentioned you've done Reiki before. So, if you have no questions, we can get started."

Tara nodded. She slipped off her shoes and laid on the table. She closed her eyes and said a silent prayer that this would clear her mind. The next hour passed quickly as Tara was taken away by relaxation and silence. She could swear she had fallen asleep, but couldn't be positive.

"Tara, we're done. Take your time." Paula kept her hand on Tara's shoulder. Tara opened her eyes and took a moment to focus. Her limbs were heavy as she tried to sit up. "Take a couple of minutes, Hun."

Tara nodded and laid back. Her eyes closed and she drifted for a moment, although hearing Paula move around the room. She opened her eyes again and focused on the wall across from her. She pulled her mind together and focused on the picture of the ocean on the wall. Her thoughts became clearer and a weightlessness filled her limbs as she sat up.

Tara stood slowly, acclimating herself to being back in the present. She moved across the room to the twin set of chairs in the corner. Her chest tightened as she sat down and faced Paula.

"How are you feeling?"

Tara closed her eyes. "Exhausted, honestly. Although, I do feel a bit less stressed."

"Tara, we need to talk about what I was feeling today."

Tara nodded and waited.

"There was an older woman here with you during your session. Do you know who that could be?"

Tara shook her head no. Slowly, she met Paula's eyes. "Maybe my grandmother. I have been having a lot of nightmares where she has been telling me to find the boy and to break the curse. I have no idea what she is talking about."

Paula reached out and grabbed Tara's hand. "She was here with you. She wants you to know that she is with you, and that you are strong enough to survive."

Tara's eyes filled with tears. "I don't know what she means."

Paula squeezed her hand. "Tara, you need to open your mind. She is trying to communicate with you, but you are shutting her out. You need to be open to what she has to say; be open to her presence."

"I don't know how." Tara's voice was a whisper.

"You have no fear from her. She is here to help you. Trust your instincts when you feel her, and let her know that you know she is with you. Let her guide her. She is insistent that it is of utmost importance that you listen to her."

Tara nodded. She thanked Paula as she stood and headed to the door. The stress had lessened, and yet she was full of more questions than she had before.

Chapter Nine

TARA ENTERED THE STAFFORD HOUSE. SHE STOPPED INSIDE THE door as she heard voices coming from the kitchen. Ryan's, she picked out immediately, but the other male voice was unknown to her.

"You know nothing about her, you are staying here with her. What are you thinking?"

"I'm thinking after being sick I wanted to be in my own bed. Besides, there is something about her...I can't explain it." Ryan's voice was soft, but held a no-nonsense tone.

"Whatever you say, dude. Your house, your rules. Just let me do what you need and get me out of this damn town."

Tara closed her eyes and a flash of a young boy crossing his arms, adamantly stating he was out of this town as soon as he was old enough. The memory was gone as quick as it came and she shook her head. It couldn't be her memory. Where were they coming from? *Gram, help me.* A warm breeze caressed her shoulders and she consciously relaxed, trying to remember to allow herself to be open to the communication from her grandmother. But she heard nothing. The warm breeze was gone as she heard the voices from the kitchen stop.

She opened her eyes and stared into those blue eyes of Ryan. "You okay?"

"Yeah, of course."

"This is Jake. Friend of mine that has a few connections that might be able to help us." Ryan gestured to the man standing beside him. "Jake, Tara."

"Nice to meet you."

Jake took a few steps closer, holding out his hand. Tara shook it and glanced curiously at the man who wanted out of this town. "Ryan didn't say how beautiful you were." He grinned at her.

Tara shrugged her shoulders. "Maybe that isn't the way he thinks." She instantly regretted the flippant reply and prayed that Ryan wouldn't try to tell her different.

Tara breathed a sigh of relief when Ryan laughed. "Perhaps it was because I didn't want Jake to start acting like an ass." He winked at Tara.

"Wonderful. Now that's the impression she has of me. I'm done. You're messing with my game, man." Jake flashed a grin once more at Tara. "Okay, tell me your life story."

Tara glanced to Ryan, panic rising up in her. "Nothing to tell, really."

"Damn, Jake, leave the girl alone." Ryan stepped over close to Tara. "We were talking about Holden House. Want to go back and look around some more?"

"Not me. That place is spooky." Jake shook his head. "I'm going to head to the Town Hall and look up records to see what we can find out about the owner.

Tara nodded. "I'm in. Give me a few minutes to shower."

Tara ran up the stairs. She was thankful Jake wasn't going to be joining them. He was fine, but there was something about him—a feeling she couldn't put her finger on. It left her unnerved. She took a quick shower, pulling on shorts and a tank top. Taking a deep breath, she tried to calm her racing heart before joining Ryan downstairs.

When Tara finally made her way back to the first floor, she found Ryan sitting in the living room by himself. "Jake gone?"

"Yeah. Were you waiting for him to leave before you came down?"

Tara laughed. "Maybe. He's a bit...aggressive."

"That's putting it nicely." Ryan joined her in the doorway. He put out his hand, waiting for her to accept it.

Tara glanced at his hand and hesitated a brief moment before locking her fingers with his. "Let's do this."

They walked in comfortable silence to the Holden House, cutting through the shortcut they had taken before. Tara briefly stopped at the side of the hole in the ground and waited for the flash of a memory, but nothing came. She had no feeling that her grandmother was with her, but a coldness ran through her that frightened her. This was a new feeling.

"You okay?" Ryan's soft voice penetrated through her thoughts, and she nodded.

They continued on and upon reaching the house, they paused at the back stairs. Tara pulled back and glanced up. "Let's make a plan of where we want to look at before we go in."

Ryan studied her. "The other day you were charging in. What's different?" Concern laced his voice.

"I don't know. I have a feeling, not a warm fuzzy feeling, but something that is...just cold."

"We don't have to do this now."

Tara squeezed his hand. "I want to. Stay close."

He pulled her close and enveloped her in a hug, warmth surrounding her, bringing her courage. "I'm not going anywhere."

They stepped apart and started up the stairs to the back door. The door creaked as they opened it and Tara hesitated before stepping into the kitchen. Gone was the warmth or the feeling of her grandmother's presence that she had previously. She stepped further into the room, looking around. Nothing had changed since the other day —not that she really had expected it to, but there was a different feeling to the house.

"Tell me you feel it too." Tara turned to face Ryan.

"Cold, ominous? Yes, I feel it." His hand tightened his grip on hers. "Do you want to go upstairs?"

Tara shook her head. "Let's go explore the servant quarters off the kitchen."

"What are you looking for? Anything specific?"

"I don't know. Just something to give me a clue as to why I feel I should be here." Tara closed her eyes and sighed. "I know it doesn't make sense. I can't verbalize it very well. There is some reason my grandmother has led me here."

Even as she spoke the words, Tara knew she sounded insane. She mentally berated herself for saying the words out loud.

"Let's do this," Ryan's voice cut through her thoughts. He stepped forward and waited for her. The minute she stepped beside him, they were off in sync, as if there were no insanity between them. Maybe there was...possibly their whole life had been insanity, and they hadn't realized they were in this together until they met.

Ryan couldn't put his finger on what it was that Tara had over him, but there was a pull of a deeper connection that he had only felt with Anna before. His memories had faded so with Anna over the years—was he projecting the feelings he had been missing on Tara and waiting for someone to love him?

As soon as they stepped down the corridor to the servant's quarters, it was like being transported back in time. Nothing had been updated in this part of the house. The wallpaper on the walls laid half off the walls, yellowed with time. Doors had been left open to the various rooms off the main corridor.

Tara approached the first one and stopped, peeking inside. The small cot in the corner still had a rough blanket over it. No pillow. The blanket had holes in it where something had chewed on it, or perhaps it had disintegrated with the years. She stepped inside and felt a coldness settle around her. She shivered and stepped forward another step.

There was an old dresser in a corner that she moved towards. She ran her hand along the top, dust flowing into the air as her hand disturbed it. She sneezed as she moved her hands to the knobs of the first drawer. It stuck as she pulled.

"Let me." Ryan was beside her. She moved aside as he gave a tug and the drawer creaked open an inch, but wouldn't budge any further.

Tara brought her face closer to the draw and peeked in. "It's too dark. I can't see anything."

Ryan pulled harder again and again, bringing out a few inches each time. Finally, with a final yank, the draw opened fully. A cloud of dust rose in front of their faces and they both waved their hands to clear it away.

As the dust settled, Tara took in the draw full of confetti—papers that had disintegrated or was a nest for a rodent of some sort. She didn't dare move her hand any closer into the mess to see if there was anything still intact to read. She took a step back as Ryan shoved the draw back into place. He yanked over the second and third draw also and they were empty.

Tara sighed and turned to glance around the room again. "What were you expecting to find?" She turned towards Ryan at the sound of his voice. She shrugged.

"I have no idea, but it's cold in here. Colder than the rest of the house. There's a presence here."

Ryan scoffed. "You really don't believe that stuff, do you?"

Tara stared at him. "Yes, I do. Very much so." The words were no sooner out of her mouth before the door slammed shut. She pointed to the door without looking at it. "What do you think that was about?"

"There's a reasonable explanation, a gust of wind..." Ryan walked to the door and turned the knob. It didn't move.

"Really? Did you feel the wind blowing in here? I certainly didn't." Tara smirked at him. "Tell me you don't feel that chill in the air. It's not a breeze; it's something or someone warning us. I felt it as soon as we entered this room, and this isn't the first time I have felt it."

"When else have you felt it?" Ryan turned and watched her.

"At the stairway, when the pictures fell off the wall."

"But only in this house?"

Tara nodded. "I feel a warm breeze. That's when I know my grandma is with me." She paused. "Look, I know you don't believe me...you think I'm crazy, but it's true."

The door opened a crack, and they both glanced at it. Ryan gestured for Tara to proceed him out of the room as he pulled it fully wide. "After you."

Tara was silent as they made their way back to the kitchen. They never got through more than one room at a time in the house before something happened. She silently cursed whoever was preventing their search of the house.

"What do you want to do?"

Tara closed her eyes, willing her grandmother to be with her. A warm breeze circled around her body. "Where, gram?" she whispered.

The warmth enveloped her and Tara felt the tension leave her shoulders. Her grandmother's voice, close to her ear, whispered, *Let him save you.* Tara's eyes flew opened and she met Ryan's stare.

"What is it?" Ryan's eyes were full of concern and Tara shook her head. It couldn't be. *Why, Gram? Why him?*

"I can't explain it. I think we should go for now, but I want to go to the basement at some point." Tara turned towards the door and hesitated. Why wait? They were here now. "Let's do it now."

"I'm not sure that's a good idea, Tara." Ryan laid his hand on her arm. "There's some freaky stuff going on here."

"I'm okay if you are with me. Trust me." Tara squeezed his hand turned towards the door leading to the basement.

Ryan grabbed her hand. "Let me go down first." She nodded and stepped aside so he could go first. Never letting go of her hand, he started down the stairs one step at a time, testing each one before putting his weight on it. The light they had flipped on flickered from time to time, and every time Ryan paused, waiting for the light to be steady again.

"You're acting like you are in a horror film." Tara laughed. "We could go a little faster down these stairs, unless you want to be here all evening."

"Don't rush me. If you want me to trust you, then you need to reciprocate that trust." He pulled her close at the bottom of the stairs.

She nodded, not trusting her voice. "I do trust you." Her voice was a whisper, but Ryan felt her relax in his arms.

"Good." He released her and took a step forward. "Where to start down here?"

Tara glanced around. The far corner housed an old fashion washer, one her grandmother must have hand-cranked to spin out the clothes. There was no dryer, just a simple wooden drying rack that was now lying on the floor. The basement floor was dirt flooring and dampness filled the place.

Just to the left of the wash area stood some plastic totes stacked against the wall. Tara pointed to them. "There."

Ryan nodded and they moved forward. The stack of totes was coated with dust. Tara stopped and stared at the totes. What was she looking for? Did she even know? *Gram, please help me.* The silent plea went unheard, as there was no warmth that surrounded her. At least the coldness hadn't returned.

Tara reached for the top tote and lifted the lid off. Ryan aimed his flashlight as they peered inside. Old bank statements and other yellowed papers filled the bin. Tara pulled out a few sheets. She pushed others aside, but there was nothing further beyond useless papers. She put the cover back on and Ryan grabbed the tote and moved it aside.

They repeated the process of looking into each tote and came up empty with each one. Although Tara wasn't sure what she was looking for, she was convinced she hadn't found anything of use at this point.

"There has to be a diary or something around to give us some sort of clue as to the history of this house." Tara sighed as they restacked the totes as they had found them.

"What sort of history do you want to know?" Ryan asked.

"I don't know. I feel like there is a story to this place, and it needs to be told." Tara shivered as a cold air settled around her. The hairs on the back of her neck stood up, and she rubbed her arms with her hands.

"Cold again?"

"She or he is back."

"Come on. You don't really believe that, do you?" Ryan put an arm around her.

"Are you telling me you don't feel the coldness?"

Ryan pulled her closer. "We are in a basement. It's cold and damp down here. We've been down here close to probably an hour and you are chilled from that."

Tara shook her head. "I know you have trouble believing this, but please, give me some credit for having a little bit of brains in my head."

"I never said you didn't..."

Tara stepped towards the stairs, out of Ryan's embrace, trying to put space between them. She put her foot up to start up the stairs.

"Tara, wait." Ryan reached for her hand, but Tara quickened her pace.

She was up about three steps when she felt the coldness tighten around her, knocking her off balance. She fell backwards, missing the banister as she reached for the railing. She hit hard against Ryan as he caught her from going all the way down, but not before a sharp pain went through her ankle as it twisted as she tried to regain her balance.

"Damn it," Tara yelled. "Is that all you have?"

"Tara." Ryan's deep voice, barely a whisper, next to her ear, calmed her a bit. "Are you okay?"

"I twisted my ankle. I'm fine."

Before she could move, Ryan slipped his arm under her knees and hauled her against his chest. He carried her the rest of the way up the stairs and outside before he set her down on the stairs of the porch. He kneeled before her and gently felt her ankle.

"It's starting to swell already. You need to have it checked." He pulled out his cell phone and punched in a number.

Tara watched him for a brief second before she closed her eyes. She fought against the tears that threatened to spill. She was pushed, but by who? And why were they trying to hurt her? She heard Ryan talking, demanding whoever he called to pick them up. She had trouble focusing on his words as a flash came to her. The same young girl falling down the cellar stairs. She was young, four or five years old. The image was gone as quickly as it came.

Tara rubbed her temples. Her head ached. Whose memories was she seeing? Was that her as a child? Her own childhood was erased from her mind...not one memory of her as a child, any birthdays, friends, even her grandmother when she was a child. *Gram, where are you?*

"Jake will be here in a couple of minutes to pick us up. You're going to the hospital to have that ankle checked."

"We can't say we were here. It's trespassing."

Ryan smiled. "We will tell the truth. You fell on the stairs. No one will ask what stairs you were on."

Tara frowned. "I'm glad one of us is finding humor in this situation."

Ryan sat down next to her. "Look, you wanted adventure. Looks like you got it."

Tara leaned her head on his shoulder. "I guess I might have to stay put for the rest of the day."

"I'm thinking you're running is down for at least the next week or so. Maybe you will get some much-needed rest."

Jake came around the corner. "I hear there is a damsel in distress back here."

"Very funny." Tara started to stand and sat back down quickly as pain shot through her ankle.

"Want me to carry you, sweetie?" Jake grinned.

"Back off, Jake." Ryan slid his arm around Tara and his other under her knees. He pulled her close and started to the car.

"Where's your white horse?" Jake laughed as Ryan casted a withering glare at him. "Oh, wait...I'm the knight in shining armor that has arrived with the ride for the fair lady."

Tara closed her eyes and smiled as Ryan's arms tightened around her.

Tara settled into the back seat with her ankle up as Jake slid behind the wheel and Ryan in the passenger front seat. She laid her head back with her eyes closed, willing herself not to cry. Her ankle throbbed, and her frustration was about to overflow. She couldn't take anymore. She wanted answers, and they were not coming. She wiped a tear away that escaped from her eye. It seemed like an eternity before Jake stopped the car.

"I'll get a wheelchair. Be right back." Ryan was out of the car before Tara could even acknowledge that she had heard him.

"How you holding up, kid?" Jake turned in his seat to look at Tara.

"I'm fine." She gave a small smile.

"Bullshit, but you keep telling yourself that." He reached back his hand and gave hers a small squeeze. "I'll park after your knight gets you into your sweet ride and takes you in."

"You don't need to stay, Jake."

"I'm thinking you're going to need a ride home when they release you. No arguments."

Tara nodded as Ryan pulled open the door. "Your chariot awaits, my dear."

Tara shook her head. "The two of you really need to stop. I don't know which of you is worse."

Tara wanted to be home in her own bed. After waiting for what seemed like eons, she was finally able to get her x-rays done and the doctor confirmed it was simply a sprain. She was to stay off it for the next few weeks, using crutches whenever she was up and about. Tara winced at the thought of trying to get around the Holden House, and especially get up and down the stairs in the Stafford House.

Finally, she was released to go home and with much fussing on the part of Ryan and Jake, she was settled back into the backseat of the car and they headed for home. Home. Such an odd way to think of a house she was renting. She really couldn't remember a place she really thought of as home. The pain medication must be getting to her. Her head was foggy, and she drifted off to sleep with her last thought being of a home with Ryan.

Tara woke briefly as Ryan helped her from the car. He picked her up again and she wrapped her arms around him, laying her head on his shoulder. Her eyes still closed, she vaguely registered the fact that he was carrying her up to bed. She felt the jolt as he kicked the bedroom door shut behind him.

"No need for Jake to come barging in," he muttered under his breath as he laid Tara gently on the bed. She tightened her arms around his neck, pulling him down. She felt him lay to the side of her and pull her close.

"Stay with me," Tara whispered as she snuggled closer.

"I'm not going anywhere." Ryan brushed her hair from away from her eyes. He gently kissed her forehead bringing a soft sigh from her lips. He closed his eyes and tried to get his mind off the warmth of her body next to his, her curves fitting perfectly against him. Her hand rested across his chest and he was sure she could feel the beat of his heart. He tried to remind himself over and over again that this was a girl that needed his help, nothing more. But reality was setting in and he knew without a doubt that she had stolen his heart and his life was never going to be the same.

Chapter Ten

TARA OPENED HER EYES SLOWLY. HER ANKLE THROBBED AND SHE was cold. She vaguely remembered Ryan sleeping next to her last night, holding her. Or was that a dream? She sat up and gingerly moved her feet to the floor. She glanced around and yet her crutches were nowhere to be found. Jake must have not brought them upstairs last night.

She had a walking boot on her foot, and although she was supposed to be using the crutches, she stepped tentatively on it. Pain shot through her foot and she sat down quickly. Tears sprang to her eyes, and she fought against the pain and the urge to break down and cry. She needed coffee and a pain pill. Determined to make it to the stairs, even if she had to crawl all the way, she hopped on her good foot to the door.

She pulled open the door and leaned against the frame to rest. She looked warily at the hallway and the stairs that appeared to be a mile away. Taking a deep breath, she started her hopping journey down the hall. She got about halfway when Ryan came up the stairs carrying a tray.

"What are you doing?" Ryan set down the tray and wrapped his arms around Tara before she lost her balance.

"I need coffee," Tara snipped.

"I have coffee for you."

"You can't keep me upstairs all the time. I want to go downstairs, get my coffee, and take a pain pill." Tara pushed against Ryan.

"Lord, woman. You do need coffee." Ryan brushed a kiss against her lips. "Jake!"

Ryan scooped up Tara and started down the stairs.

Jake came out of the kitchen sipping his coffee. "You called?"

"Watch out. The lady of the house is wanting her coffee and she is miserable before she has it."

Tara slightly smacked Ryan. "I am not. I don't invalid well."

Ryan snickered. "No, you don't."

Tara settled into the chair at the kitchen table as Jake slid a coffee mug in front of her. He backed away with his arms up in mock surrender. "You both need to stop this ridiculousness." She closed her eyes and inhaled her coffee, allowing the rich aroma to soothe her frazzled nerves before she took that first sip.

She hated to admit it, but once the caffeine hit her system, she felt an instant change in her mood. Oh, how she hated to be that person that couldn't function without coffee, but there was no doubt she was that poor soul. She glanced around.

"Need a pain pill?" Ryan filled a glass with water for her and brought her prescription to her.

"Are you going to wait on me hand and foot all day?"

Tara asked before popping the pill in her mouth and swallowing, chasing it down with half of the water.

"For the day? Honey, we are at your beck and call for the next few weeks. You are going to remain off that foot," Ryan said, bowing before her.

"Stop. Enough of this. I'm not going to be laid up for the next few weeks. I agree to stay put today and possibly tomorrow. Beyond that there is no guarantee." Tara sipped her coffee again.

The room was silent. Tara glanced up to see both Jake and Ryan staring at her. She shook her head and pointed from one to the other. "Don't even think of it. Don't either one of you dare to tell me what I'm going to be doing. Where are my crutches?"

Ryan pointed to the counter over by the kitchen door. "Do you want them?"

Tara took in the distance to the door and then back to Ryan. "Fine, can you get them for me?" Not a word was said as Tara gulped down the rest of her coffee and hobbled out of the room. She got to the bottom of the stairs, looked up and proceeded to the living room where she settled on the couch, propping her ankle up on a pillow. She felt the pain pill start to kick in and she drifted off to sleep.

Unsure how long she had been sleeping, Tara snuggled down under the blanket. With a vague awareness, she knew Ryan had covered her. That man was determined to kill her with kindness and it irked her that she was enjoying the idea of being pampered by him. She had practically begged him to stay with her last night and shamelessly snuggled up against him, wishing her ankle hadn't bothered her because she wanted nothing more last night than to feel him against her, skin on skin. But in true Ryan form, he had been a perfect gentleman, which endeared him even more to her.

Ryan sat in the chair across from the couch, watching Tara sleep. She was restless, and he glanced for the hundredth time at his watch. She had been sleeping about three hours and he knew that she would be due for another pain pill soon. She was not going to be happy when she found out that he and Jake had made a plan. Jake was going back to the Holden House to do a search. Jake believed, like Tara, in ghosts, but also felt that he was better equipped to deal with whatever was over there than Ryan. Ryan was thrilled about not having to go back to the house anytime soon.

Lost in his own thoughts, he realized that Tara was watching him. "Welcome back to the land of the living."

"How long have I been sleeping?" Tara pushed herself up to a sitting position.

Ryan stood and helped reposition the pillow under her ankle. "About three hours. Hungry?"

Tara nodded. Ryan felt her eyes on him, but he couldn't bring himself to make eye contact with her.

"What is it?" Tara asked.

"What?" Ryan looked down at her. "What would you like to eat?"

Tara reached for his hand and pulled him down in front of her. "Ryan, why are you avoiding me?"

"I'm not. I'm just worried about you. You're stubborn as hell, and I know you are not going to let this ankle heal."

Tara watched him. "Nice try, but I'm not buying it. I'll let it go for now."

Ryan leaned into her, capturing her mouth. His tongue teased her until she gave a soft moan and entwined her fingers in the hair at the base of his neck. He angled her as she pulled him closer, gaining greater access to that mouth that he couldn't get enough of. His hand slid up her side, coming to rest as he cupped her breast, his thumb brushing back and forth over her nipple. He pulled back slightly and looked into her eyes. The need and want was there, staring back at him, matching his own need and want for her. He knew if they continued, he would soon be at the point of no return and she was in no physical condition to let this continue.

"Ryan?" The soft question was like a punch to his gut.

"Not like this, Tara. I want you fully functioning when we take this further." He winked at her and stood before she could hold him there. "I'll get you something to eat." He escaped the living room, trying desperately to ignore the look of hurt in her eyes.

He was a coward. He busied himself in the kitchen making sandwiches. He prayed that by the time Jake got back, Tara would be asleep again and they could talk without her knowing. Ryan didn't know what to expect, and he didn't believe in ghosts, but something odd was definitely going on at the Holden House.

He put their lunches on a tray along with another pain pill for Tara and started to the living room. He paused in the foyer as he heard Tara talking.

"I don't know what is going on, but I need some answers."

Was she on the phone? He tiptoed to the living room door and, as far as he could tell, Tara wasn't on her phone. She was sitting there with her head back against a pillow, eyes closed. Had she gone back to sleep? "Lunch is served."

Tara gave him a small smile. "Thank you, Ryan. I

really appreciate you helping me like this. I'm sure this isn't what you expected when you came home to rest."

Ryan handed her a plate and sat down on the floor, his back against the couch. "No, not what I was expecting, but I'm enjoying it surprisingly enough."

Tara snorted and Ryan tried not to grin as he took a bite of his sandwich. They ate in silence. When they were done and plates were on the tray, off to the side, Ryan turned to Tara. "I want to understand. Tell me about the feelings you have when your grandmother is with you."

"You admit my grandmother is with me?"

Ryan smiled. "Yes, because you told me she is. I don't know if I believe in ghosts or spirits, but you obviously do, and God knows Jake does."

Tara nodded. "I don't know if I can explain it, but I feel a warmth around me when she is with me. I hear her voice whisper in my ear, or she is in my dreams telling me what to do, where to go...it's how I came to this town, to find Holden House." Tara closed her eyes and took a deep breath.

"What about the coldness at the Holden House?"

Tara opened her eyes and watched Ryan. "I know you don't believe me, but there is a chilling air about me when I feel the presence there. It's not a good presence. Someone is angry and wants to hurt someone. I don't know if they are specifically looking to hurt me, or if they are trying to stop us from searching the house, but there is something. When I fell yesterday, I felt the cold air pushing against me. It was like I was pushed backwards down the stairs."

"What? You think that wasn't just a misstep?" Ryan sat up tall.

Tara shook her head. "No. It was deliberate. The question is why, and am I really the target or is it just being in the right place at the wrong time?"

"You're not going back there then."

Tara put up her hand. "Really? You are going to stop me from going back based on something you don't even believe in. Come on."

"I don't care if I believe it or not. I don't want you hurt." Ryan stood and grabbed the tray.

"Don't you run away while we're talking. I will hobble after you." Tara stood.

"I'm not running away. I'm frustrated. Do you not get how important you are to me?" He set the tray on the end table, reaching a hand to help Tara stand.

Tara froze. Important to him? Ryan stepped close to her, holding her close. "Tara, you have weaseled your way into my heart and I don't know how to fight it anymore."

She leaned into his embrace, her head on his chest. "Were you trying to fight it?"

He nodded. "As much as you are trying to fight it."

She allowed herself to relax against him. He was right she was fighting it and why? Because everything was so unsure in her life right now – but maybe he was the stability she sought after. Her grandmother approved obviously.

"Are you going to continue to be on that foot, or are you going to sit down and relax?" Ryan made no move to step away.

"I'm going to rest, but I need a change of scenery. I think I'll go out on the porch for a while." Tara reached for her crutches, but clung to Ryan's shoulders instead as he easily lifted her into his arms and started for the door. "You have to stop doing that."

"Why? I enjoy holding you." He settled her into a

rocker on the porch and pulled another chair up in front of her to prop her ankle up on.

"Thank you." Tara inhaled deeply the fresh air. She felt like she had been in a fog since yesterday. She winced as she moved her foot to get more comfortable.

"Did you take your pain pill?"

Tara shook her head and shrugged. "I'll try just some ibuprofen for the pain. I don't like the fogginess from the pain pills. I would prefer to sleep tonight instead of all day."

Chapter Eleven

JAKE MANEUVERED HIS CAR TO THE BACK OF THE HOUSE AND SAT there. This place had always given him the creeps. He hated being here as a kid, yet Ryan and Anna insisted on always playing in the woods around this house. Until Anna kept getting hurt. Jake had always felt there was a bigger issue going on with those accidents, but he was too young to know.

Now he was a PI and had done a lot of studying on paranormal activity. He knew Tara felt there was a spirit in this house and he was half hoping he would run into it today. With a sigh, he opened the car door and began the short trek to the back porch.

He entered the house through the kitchen, just as Ryan had instructed him to do. Ryan had no clue what it was Tara was searching for, but he was hoping to find some sort of personal papers that would lead him to the heir of the house. Ryan had filled him in on the servant quarters already being searched and the basement. He started to the front of the house and came into the foyer with the staircase winding up the side of the foyer to the second floor. He felt a cool breeze brush against him as he started to the stairs.

"Got something to show me, honey?" He taunted the stillness of the house. He felt like he had drunk a dozen espressos as he started up to the second floor. The chill in the air intensified as he got closer to the second floor. He paused at the top of the stairs. He ran his hand along the banister and looked down to the front door. He was freezing now and shivered as he tucked his hands in his pockets, trying to warm them. *Damn, something bad must've happened here.* He turned towards the hallway that ran the length of the second floor.

He remembered Ryan had mentioned being in the bedroom with the dollhouse and how it had triggered some sort of flashback for Tara. He decided to start at the other side of the hall and see what those rooms held.

The first door he opened was empty. No furniture, nothing. The windows were even naked of any window dressings. He shut the door and continued to the next room. He swung open the door and realized the coldness had left him. He stepped into the room. He felt like he was stepping back in a time warp.

The canopy bed was covered with a heavy velvet bed robe. The canopy, although worn thin with just years of disintegration, was still in place. This room obviously was the master room. There was a chair over by a fireplace and beyond that was a door half open that led to the dressing room. Jake ventured into the room further, glancing around looking for something that could hold papers. There was no desk or dresser. He pulled the dressing room door open fully and walked into a closet that could have been another room. Rods hung on the sides to hold clothes, but they were empty, and in the right back corner stood a small vanity. The table was littered with dried up make-up, empty perfume bottles, as well as a stylish hair comb. He wondered how many years this stuff had just been here – long before the old lady of this haunted house was here he would imagine.

One drawer was in the center of the table and he pulled it gently open. Hair pins littered the bottom of the drawer and nothing else. He breathed a sigh of relief that there was nothing else, although he wasn't sure why he was relieved. This whole room, suite if you would, just had a sad air about it. It was stifling the oppressiveness he felt in here and he suddenly felt the urge to get some fresh air. He turned on his heel and left the dressing room. The bedroom door was closed. He stopped short when he realized he had left it opened.

The room was empty. There was no place for someone to hide. He felt a chilly breeze around him again. "What do you want? Is this your room?" he shouted. The door burst open and banged against the wall. Jake bolted from the room and stopped short in the hallway. He turned back towards the room. He blinked again and again as he tried to focus on the chair by the fireplace. Was there really a woman sitting there, crying? He rubbed his eyes with his fists and looked again. The room was empty.

He nodded, muttering to himself. "Okay, someone has hurt you and you're upset. Tell me who you are." He turned towards the next closed door down the hallway. He took a deep breath and opened the door. Another empty room, a lot smaller than the others. This one looked to have never been used.

He moved on to the next. As soon as he opened the door, there was a warmth in the room that soothed him.

The window shades were open and the sun shined through the grimy window. The bed was a smaller, simpler bed with a handmade quilt covering it. It was worn, but still in good shape. A three-drawer dresser stood in the corner. Jake moved slowly towards it, mindfully aware of his surroundings. No cold air, just warmth. The hurt lady obviously didn't frequent this room. He sighed a breath of relief.

Upon opening the first drawer, he found remnants of clothing. Something had obviously been eating their way through them, or nesting in them. He pushed the drawer in and moved to the second one. More of the same. He pulled open the third drawer and found an old tin.

He picked up the tin and sat on the edge of the bed with it. Dust settled around him as he sat there just holding the tin. Did he want to open it or should he just take the whole thing with him to Ryan and Tara? What if it didn't hold anything? He didn't want to get Tara's hopes up and crush them with the fact that it was empty. Using his thumbs, he pushed open the lid.

Jackpot! Inside was an envelope with one simple word on the front of it. *Ryan*. His Ryan? He turned the envelope over, and although sealed originally, the seal had obviously dried out and could easily be opened. Should he read it? He set it aside and look into the tin again. Photographs lined the bottom of the tin. All pictures of Anna before she moved, Anna and Ryan, and even one with Jake in it with Anna and Ryan. One of those rare occasions Jake had actually come to the house with them.

What was the connection between Holden House and Tara? Jake put the pictures back in the tin and put the cover on it. He slipped the envelope for Ryan into his pocket. He would take the tin with him, and he had had enough for the day. Although he felt calm in this room, he knew he had to transverse through the hallway and down the stairs, the part of the house that had him freezing on the way in.

He squared his shoulders and started for the stairs. He glanced in the master suite as he walked by – empty. He was down the stairs and outside before he realized that the coldness had never returned. Had she had enough once she revealed herself crying to Jake? Was that all he needed to know today was that someone was heart-broken in that house? He needed to do some in-depth research and find out the story of this house from the beginning of the walls being built until Anna disappeared.

Jake pulled up in front of the Stafford House. Ryan and Tara were sitting on the porch talking. Ryan stood as Jake got out of the car.

"Looky here." Jake waved the tin. He took the steps to the porch two at a time and handed the tin off to Ryan. Ryan sat next to Tara and they opened it. As they were looking at the pictures, Tara was stunned.

"Who are these kids?"

Ryan pointed to the picture. "That's me, Anna...and this one even has Jake in it."

"Who was the lady that owned the house?" Tara moved her head from side to side, feeling the tension release as she moved.

"It was Anna's grandmother that lived there," Ryan answered. "We were only there a few times. I'm not sure of her name."

Jake shrugged. "It was creepy then and definitely creepier now."

"See any ghosts?" Ryan joked.

Jake looked at Ryan and then to Tara. Tara's eyes were fixated on him. He nodded. "Yes, as a matter of fact I did."

"Get out!" Ryan sat back in the chair and propped his feet up on the railing.

Jake knocked his feet down. "I'm not kidding, man. There was a ghost in one of the rooms crying."

"Do you know who she was?" Tara sat up, intrigued.

"Come on, man. Stop feeding her this crap." Ryan shook his head.

"Ryan, how can you not believe this? Spirits are around us all the time; most are harmless and are meant to comfort us. There are a few that are angry or hurt and take it out on those they come in contact with." Tara reached for his hand. She willed him to believe her and Jake. She needed him to open his mind to the possibilities.

"Tara, I just don't get it. I can't believe in something I can't physically see and touch." He squeezed her hand gently. "Don't be offended by that."

"And vice versa...don't be offended at what we believe or mock it."

Ryan nodded. "Go ahead, Jake. Tell us what you found."

Jake turned towards Tara and directed his commentary towards her. "There was an ice cold feeling in the foyer and it got colder as I made my way up the stairs to the second floor. It was downright brutally cold at the top of the stairs and I lingered there for a moment, running my hand on the railing. It was like touching a block of ice."

Tara nodded. She was on the edge of her seat, waiting to hear more.

He continued, "The master bedroom, or suite as there was an attached dressing room to it I think was hers. I left the door open when I went into the room. I ventured into the dressing room and when I came out, the bedroom door was shut. Man, there was still make-up on her table in the dressing room. Like it was just left alone and never cleaned after she died."

"Do you think she died in the house?"

"I think it's possible. She was dressed in a long dress, like hundreds of years ago. She was young though. I didn't get a good look at her, but when I got to the hallway and looked back into the room she was sitting in the chair by the fireplace crying. I mean really weeping."

Tara's eyes filled with tears. "Oh, I wonder what could have caused her such pain."

"Wait a minute." Ryan glanced from Jake to Tara. "You are not going on another different wild goose chase now. This has nothing to do with what your grandmother is trying to tell you."

Tara turned towards Ryan. "How do you know? What if it is all related? I need to know who she is and when she lived here...how she died. There must be some sort of records somewhere. Historical Society maybe?"

"That would be a good place to start. I'll call them and see if we can get any information on the house when it was first built and the first owners. Then we can go from there." Jake stood. "Okay. I'll let you know what I find out. You really should get some rest, my lady." He bowed at the waist and shot Tara a grin as he slapped Ryan on the shoulder as he walked past him.

Chapter Twelve

RYAN SANK INTO THE RECLINER AND SIGHED. TARA HAD SETTLED down for a nap with her foot elevated on a pillow on the couch. Ryan watched her sleeping, her breathing even and deep. Her chest rising and falling with each breath was mesmerizing. He couldn't help but wonder what could have happened in her life so that she had no memories of her childhood years. He would be lost without his memories of Anna growing up.

He held on to those memories for so long now; he sometimes wondered if the memories were really as good as the reality had been or had he built it up in his mind because he wanted to remember it being wonderful with his best friend. He could picture her so vividly in his mind's eye. He would never forget the laughter or the way she would reach for his hand while wanting him to tag along on an adventure.

He closed his eyes and he could see Anna laughing at his jokes. The way her eyes sparkled when she laughed. She was the only one whose eyes sparkled and truly showed her joy. Or was she? Ryan opened his eyes and looked at Tara. He had seen that sparkle in her when she let herself go and actually enjoyed herself.

Maybe he was just attracted to the same type of woman...although Anna was a child when she moved away. He shook his head and stood. He needed to clear his mind. He wrote a brief note to Tara stating he was going for a walk. He had no sooner set foot outside the door when his phone vibrated with a text coming in from Jake.

"Meet me. Have something for you. Didn't want Tara to see it."

Ryan replied, *"Corner of Hawthorne and Maple, 5 mins."*

When Ryan arrived at the street corner, Jake was leaning against his car waiting for him. "'Bout time you got here."

"I said five minutes." Ryan glanced at his watch. "It's been four."

Jakes grinned. "Didn't want to tear you away from your girl."

Ryan shook his head. "What do you have for me?"

Jake held out an envelope. "Found this at the house. Thought it was strange it was addressed to you."

Ryan took the envelope and saw the single word *Ryan* on the front. "Are you sure it's for me?"

"I don't know any other Ryan's, do you?"

"No, but that doesn't mean there isn't one." Ryan stared at the envelope.

"Just open it already."

Ryan flipped it over and saw the seal was dried out and opened. "Did you read it?"

Jake shook his head no. "Not addressed to me."

Ryan pulled out the piece of paper and opened it up. He started reading.

Ryan, I miss you so much. I can't believe mom and dad moved me away from you. They tell me I will forget you in time, but I won't. I promise you, I won't. On my 25th birthday I promise I will meet you at my grandmother's house (watch out for the hole). I'm sending this to gram, hoping she will get this letter to you. I miss you so much. Love always, Anna XOXO

Anna. How many years ago did she write this? Why didn't he ever get it? She would be twenty-five this year....in a few days. Could he really see her again? His mind reeled with the possibilities that tore through it. Then one word stopped it all. Tara.

"Dude, what are you going to do?" Jake's voice broke through Ryan's thoughts.

"I don't know." Ryan stared at the paper. "I never thought I would see her again, not after we couldn't find her."

"Kismet?"

"I don't know." Ryan looked up at Jake. "What about Tara?"

"What about her? She rents your grandfather's house, your house...is there something there?" Jake winked.

"Seriously, man. I don't know how I feel. I'm attracted to her...there is something about her that just...I can't explain it."

"What does it hurt to go meet Anna? Anna and you could end up just friends and nothing more. Dude, it's been more than a decade."

"I suppose. I just feel like she should have been the one."

Jake snorted in disgust. "Come on, man. You two were kids. You were too young to know if she was the one or not. Maybe Tara is the one for you."

Ryan nodded. "I've got a few days to think about it." He turned toward home and stopped. "What did you find at the historical society about the house?"

"Still waiting on a return call." Jake placed a hand on Ryan's shoulder. "Go home to her and relax. Listen to your instincts."

Ryan glanced back at Jake and gave a brief nod of the head before he started home. The letter he folded and slipped into his back pocket of his jeans. This was something he had always longed for and now that he was faced with the opportunity, he didn't know if he really wanted to know what he still felt for Anna.

Go home to her. Those words resonated with him with every step he took. He was practically jogging by the time he reached the steps to the porch. He took the stairs two at a time and stopped short when he reached the front door. He opened the door quietly in hopes that Tara was still sleeping. He was just closing it when he heard her voice calling from the living room.

"I'm awake. No need to be quiet."

He approached the living room to find her sitting up on the couch, her foot still elevated, but a book in her lap with her eyes trained on the opening to the living room, waiting for him.

"I didn't want to wake you."

"I'm awake. I can't sleep all day long. I will never sleep tonight with the amount of napping I have already done."

Ryan chuckled. "Like you sleep at night anyway."

Tara grinned at him. "But still..."

"Still what? We will be up, having coffee at some ungodly hour because you can't sleep. What will be so different about that?" Ryan lifted her foot and slid onto the couch next to her, laying her leg over his knees.

"How was your walk?"

Ryan shrugged. "Okay, I guess." He fought the urge to tell her about the letter. Instead, he reached for her hand and laced his fingers with hers.

"You okay?" Tara's voice was soft as her thumb made small circles on Ryan's hand.

"Yeah. It's been a long day, I guess. Just worn out."

"What can I do to help?" Tara's eyes searched his, looking for something and Ryan wasn't sure what.

He shook his head. "I'm good. I'm here for you, remember?"

Tara squeezed his hand. "We're here for each other. It's a two-way street."

Ryan leaned his head back and closed his eyes. There was a comfort on those words and yet he didn't want to read too much into them. They had known each other simply days and yet there was this pull between them, guiding them to each other. Did he really believe this stuff? He was overtired and too many ghost stories were flying around for his mind to be clear. "I could use a nap myself."

———

Tara watched Ryan. He was so unassuming as he sat there with his head laid back against the couch, eyes closed. She hadn't been able to stop the words before they left her mouth, and yet she was comforted by them herself. Deep down, she knew her grandmother would be so proud of her. She could feel it was the right move. What she couldn't figure out was why there was such a connection between the two. Why she wanted Ryan so much to continue to be a part of her life regardless of what they found out about the house or the ghost.

Tara cleared her mind and silently cried out to her grandmother. *I need direction, Gram! Where do I go from here? What are you trying to tell me?* A softness brushed her cheek and Tara closed her eyes knowing her grandmother was with her. *Talk to me, Gram.*

Instinctively Tara tightened her grip on Ryan's hand. She took a deep breath in and held it for a heartbeat while she willed her grandmother to talk to her.

"What is it?"

She shook her head. She could feel Ryan's eyes on her and her frustration grew. "Nothing. I have nothing."

"What do you mean?" Puzzlement was clear in Ryan's voice.

"I just want to know what my grandmother wants to tell me. I can't seem to connect with her." A lone tear escaped from Tara's eye and rolled down her cheek. She opened her eyes when she felt Ryan brush it away. His fingers lingered on her cheek, a soft caress that calmed her. "We need to go back to the house."

"No. Not until we have some information from the historical society about who lived there. You get hurt there every time and if the ghost is trying to hurt you..." Ryan shuddered.

Tara playfully punched him in the shoulder. "I thought you didn't believe in ghosts."

"Let's just say, maybe you have opened my mind a little bit. I'm not sure I believe in ghosts, but I don't want to take chances with your life either."

Tara bit her bottom lip and watched him. His eyes were focused on her lip and she leaned towards him. He murmured, "Do you know what you do to me" just before he captured her lips with his, and his tenderness overwhelmed her. She leaned into the kiss and sighed softly, returning his passion.

She pulled back from the kiss and searched his eyes. "I love that you care about me, but I need answers."

"I don't want to see any harm come to you."

"You'll be with me."

Ryan groaned. "That's unfair and you know it. Besides you can't do the stairs with the crutches."

"I'll manage. You could carry me." The smile that tugged at the corner of her mouth was infectious and Tara knew the moment Ryan caved.

Chapter Thirteen

TARA'S MIND WAS CLEAR, HAVING STOPPED TAKING THE PAIN medication for her ankle. She maneuvered pretty well on the crutches. She had convinced Ryan that she was able to move around the "haunted house" as she was starting to refer to it by now. All she knew is she wanted answers.

Jake was supposed to meet them there and the three of them would search together. It was the only condition Ryan had for her to be able to go – Jake would be there too in case something happened. Tara almost felt giddy with anticipation as they pulled up to the house. Jake had arrived before them and was waiting on the back steps.

"It's about time you got here." Jake stood as they came around the corner.

"Ryan was dragging his feet." Tara grinned. She put both her crutches in one hand and started hopping up the back steps.

"Can't you wait two seconds for help?" Ryan rushed over to her and grabbed the crutches.

"Don't need help. Stop fretting."

Jake swung open the back door for Tara to pass

through as she hopped across the threshold, refusing to get the crutches back from Ryan. "He's like an old lady wrought with worry."

Tara giggled at Jake's tone as she leaned against the kitchen counter. A warm breeze surrounded her, and a peace settled around her shoulders. *Where to, Gram?*

A slamming door coming from upstairs caused the three of them to jump. Tara glanced over at the guys. Jake had fascination written all over his face whereas Ryan looked like he was ready to bolt any second.

"Shall we check it out?" Tara reached for the crutches.

"You want to go to the second floor on crutches?" Ryan held onto them.

Tara simply stared at him until he slowly let go. She adjusted herself and started moving forward towards the front of the house following Jake and Ryan close behind her. Jake stopped at the foot of the stairs and looked up.

Tara felt Ryan's hand on the small of her back and she glanced over to him. "I'm not sure this is a good idea," he whispered.

"Don't be a wimp. I'll protect you." Tara leaned over and kissed him on the cheek.

"Let's go you two love birds." Jake started up the starts.

Ryan swung Tara into his arms and started up the stairs behind Jake. Halfway up the stairs, a cold air settled around them. Ryan slowed and Tara tightened her arms around his neck, banging her crutches into his head.

"Sorry." She held the crutch out away from him. "Do you feel that?"

Ryan nodded. "That's not your grandmother, I take it?"

"No." Tara closed her eyes and focused. *Who are you? Talk to me please.*

Ryan let her legs drop slowly as he arrived at the top of the stairwell. Jake was staring into the first bedroom. "Is she there, Jake?"

"I can't see her, but she's here with us." Jake turned towards Tara. "Can you feel her?"

"Yes." Tara moved forward, hobbling with her crutches the best she could, towards the room. She glanced into it and saw nothing, but the cold air around her was colder and she shivered.

"How can it be getting colder in here?" Ryan spoke just behind Tara, causing her to jump.

"She's close by and not happy about us being here."

Him.

Tara paused. "You're not happy with *him* being here?"

Jake turned towards Tara. "Which one of us is she not happy with?"

Tara shrugged. "I don't know."

Ryan suddenly kneeled beside Tara. His hands held his head and he doubled over.

"Dude, what's going on?"

"My head...it's killing me." Ryan rocked forward.

"Stop it!" Tara yelled. "Let him be."

"Why? Why is it me?" Ryan sat upright, still holding his head. "It's lessened now."

Tara took a step towards the bedroom. "Talk to me. Why are you doing this?"

Crying filled the air around him. All three of them looked around, but couldn't pinpoint the direction in which it came. *He did this!* The words were riddled with anguish and Tara felt the heartache pierce through her as the sobbing continued.

"What did he do to you?" Tara's voice was compassionate and saddened. She could feel the physical pain shoot through her like a knife to her heart.

He doesn't love you. He didn't love me.

"Who didn't love you? Was it your boyfriend, your husband?" Tara begged for answers. "Tell me your name at least."

Cecilia. Don't fall for it.

"Fall for what? Don't go." A warmth spread over Tara and she knew her grandmother had allowed the conversation. She glanced over at Ryan and Jake who were just watching her. "Did you not hear her?"

Both of them shook their heads no. "It's warmer though and my head doesn't hurt." Ryan spoke, his voice laced with worry. "What did she say?"

Tears flooded Tara's eyes and her resolve broke. She sobbed like Cecilia had been sobbing. Everything within her that she had held down for all these years broke through and she couldn't control the tears and the heart-wrenching sobs that broke from her. Jake and Ryan were at her side in a heartbeat.

"What is it, Tara?" Ryan wrapped his arms around her.

"It's the residual from the ghost. Tara's emotions are portraying hers," Jake stated.

"What does that mean?" Ryan demanded.

"It's okay. It means the ghost allowed Tara to feel her, to allow her to know what was going on." Jake grabbed the crutches and handed them to Ryan. He picked up Tara effortlessly and started down the starts. "Let's get her home."

Fury ran through Ryan as he watched Jake walk away with his girl. His girl? The jealousy tore through him before he realized what it was. This house evoked such intense emotions. He could care less if he ever stepped foot in here again. He started after Jake at a jog to catch up. He didn't stop until they were at the car and he actually could feel like himself again.

"We are not going back in there again." Ryan declared when Tara was settled into the front seat.

"Dude, relax. We need answers." Irritation rolled over Ryan at the sound of Jake's voice.

"It wasn't you dropping to your knees in pain. It wasn't you bursting into tears because of a ghost's emotions. You don't get to tell me to relax." Ryan clenched his fists at his side, holding back the urge to deck his best friend.

"Ryan." Tara's soft voice broke through the anger. "It's not Jake you're mad at. It's her, Cecilia. But there has to be a reason for her behavior. We need to find the answers."

"Not here we don't. I don't care if you talk to the historical society, a psychic, whatever, but I don't want you back in there."

Tara gave him a small smile. "It's not your choice and please don't make me choose between you and finding answers."

"Tara..." Ryan stopped and knew he had been beaten. There was no way she was going to listen to him. Whatever emotions this ghost awakened in her, it was not endearing to him. He could either support her or alienate himself from her. The latter was not something he intended to do.

They drove home in silence. Jake had decided to follow-up on the historical society and was going to try and track down one of the people involved to get a face-to-face discussion about the house. Ryan stewed and ran through scenarios in his mind of how he could get Tara to back off from this insanity. He could only imagine what was going through her mind and he left him feeling discombobulated and completely off-kilter.

After parking the car, Ryan went around to open Tara's door. He reached in to help her and, although she took his hand, she was distant and quiet. He helped her stand, but stood in front of her so she couldn't take a step.

"Don't shut me out, please."

She locked eyes with his. "I'm not shutting you out. I'm tired, and I don't want you telling me what to do."

"I'm sorry." Ryan wanted nothing more than to pull her in his arms, but he held back. "It was instinct. It scared me what happened there."

"I know. It is scary, but now you have to believe in ghosts."

Ryan took a step backwards. Is this what it had come down to? Just his belief in whether the ghost was real or not? He was concerned about Tara and her wellbeing. He didn't give a damn about some dead woman who was wreaking havoc with his life or Tara's.

"I see your mind going. Ryan, I care for you, I do. But I have to follow this through."

He nodded and handed her crutches to her. He forced himself to watch her move slowly towards the house and felt like a heel for letting her go instead of just picking her up and carrying her to bed. He was exhausted himself and wanted nothing more than to wrap his arms around her and allow them both to sleep in the safety of each other's love. Love? Did he love her?

More than ever his own emotions were all over the place. He was torn between a love he had built up in his mind for Anna and the real emotions that coursed through him for this woman in front of him, in flesh and blood, that could actually love him in return. Why was there even a question of where his focus should be?

Chapter Fourteen

By the time Ryan had entered the house, Tara was settled upstairs on her bed with her laptop on her legs. She was exhausted, but more intrigued than anything. Cecilia. It couldn't be that hard to trace a name in this town, even if it was hundreds of years old. She had no timeframe and only a first name.

The Holden House. Was Cecilia a Holden? Tara immediately pulled up Google and typed in Cecilia Holden. No results. She typed in Holden House and up came the house itself and a story about the haunting of it, speculation and that was it. There were no links to previous owners or even the most recent owner. She paused and tried to think through what would be the next logical search.

A soft knock on her door brought her attention back to the present. It opened slowly before she could answer and Ryan stuck his head in. "You okay?"

She nodded and patted the bed beside her. "Want to join me?"

Ryan came in and laid down beside her, looking up at her. "You're searching for her, aren't you?"

Tara smiled down at him. "You know me so well."

Ryan chuckled. "It's a curse."

Tara closed her laptop and set it aside. She snuggled down flush next to Ryan. "What do you think about today? Honestly, how bad was the headache?"

Ryan pulled her close into his arms and nuzzled her neck. "It was pretty intense. I've never felt anything like that before."

"I know it was a different sensation for you, and I know you haven't believed before, but..." Tara twisted around to face him. "What do you think now?"

"You're not going to just rest until we have this conversation, are you?"

She shook her head no.

Ryan rolled to his back. "I think there was something supernatural going on there. I'm not sure what to believe. I didn't hear anything, but you obviously did. Jake didn't hear it, but he saw her before. I don't know what to think." Ryan took a deep breath and exhaled it slowly. "Tell me about what you heard, what you felt."

Tara rested her head on his chest. His heartbeat was steady and thumbed rhythmically against her. It brought a sense of oneness to her. "She was sobbing, I mean, heartbroken sobbing. It was disconcerting. I've never heard anyone cry like that before. It broke my heart, Ry."

Ryan wrapped his arms around her and held her. His hand slowly moved up and down her arm.

"Someone, a man, really hurt her. I just don't know if it was physically or just emotionally. She's upset with you for that reason. Either you remind her of him or she thinks you are going to hurt me. I don't know. I need to know what happened to her."

"Where was your grandmother in all this? Why wasn't she protecting us from this?"

Tara raised her head and looked at Ryan. "I know this will sound strange, but I think Gram was allowing the conversation and interaction to happen. I think she probably was thinking it would give us some insight on what it is she wants us to find."

"I don't understand any of this."

"I know, I don't really either. But I know I feel my grandmother and I'm at peace with searching for Cecilia's information because I think she needs some peace herself."

Ryan pulled her close and kissed her forehead. "I trust you. I'll try not to get protective, but I don't want to see you get hurt."

"Thank you. That means a lot and I promise I won't intentionally put myself in harm's way. But you have to admit, it is exciting trying to figure out all the clues."

Ryan groaned. "My wannabe sleuth...you will probably be the death of me."

Tara smiled. His. She liked the sound of that.

She drifted off to sleep with a smile on her face and a contentment in her heart that hadn't been there for as long as she could remember. In sleep, life became a little too real.

The girl was looking out the back window of the car, tears streaming down her face, waving frantically. She was yelling to someone that she didn't want to go. Don't let them take me.

Tara sat up screaming. Ryan reached for her. "What is it?"

"I don't know. Another dream." Tara shivered. "It was

so real...a small girl. I don't know who it is. It's the same girl that is in all my dreams."

Ryan glanced at the clock. It was close to five. "Come on. I'll make coffee and omelets. We'll talk it through."

"Yes, to the food and coffee. No, I don't want to talk it through. I want to forget the dreams."

Ryan scooped her up in his arms to carry her downstairs. "No, you don't, because you know somehow this is all connected and you want all the clues you can get."

She sighed as she settled against his chest. "You know you don't have to carry me."

"Shhh...I think I do. Please don't rain on my parade of holding you close."

Tara snuggled closer. "Hold me anytime you want."

He parked her at the kitchen table and moved around the kitchen puttering getting dinner together while the coffee brewed. Tara sat in silence at the table, and Ryan swore he could see the gears turning in her mind as she tried to figure out the dream. He was quiet, letting her work through things until the food was ready.

By the time he slid a plate of food in front of her, outwardly she appeared calmer. He watched her dig into the food with gusto. She never ceased to amaze him with her love for food. She wasn't shy about shoveling the food in and grinned at him as he watched her eat.

"Your food is getting cold." She pointed to his plate with her fork.

He chuckled as he started eating. She certainly wasn't embarrassed about eating in front of him, which he adored. He always hated it when girls would barely eat around a guy because they were afraid of spilling something.

"Tell me about your dream."

Tara shook her head no. "Let's not talk about it."

Ryan sat back, holding his coffee mug. "Come on, you know we need to talk this through."

"You don't believe in all this so why does it matter?"

"Back to that. It really doesn't matter what I believe at this point. These dreams keep plaguing you and if we can figure out why, then maybe they will stop."

"It's like it's someone else's memories."

Ryan sat forward in his chair. "How do you know they aren't your memories? You said yourself you have no recollection of your life when you were little."

Tara pulled her hair back into a ponytail, wrapping the elastic around her wrist around her hair. "I don't know. I don't know anything at this point." Frustration laced her words. Tears filled her eyes and she blinked hard to keep them from overflowing her lashes.

Ryan reached his hand across the table for hers. "We'll figure it out together."

"I think I'll take a shower. Maybe that will clear my head." She raised her hand at him when he stood to help her. "I've got this."

Ryan slid back into his chair. He wanted to argue, but the sheer determination on her face made him think twice about pushing the issue. She slowly hobbled towards the door to the kitchen, using just her toes of her hurt foot. He had to admire her strength.

Chapter Fifteen

Ryan cleaned the kitchen while Tara was upstairs. He poured another cup of coffee and made his way out to the porch. The sun was just coming up. Turning his focus to the happenings at the Holden House, Ryan logically couldn't support the idea of a ghost playing with him. However, the intense pain in his head was real. He didn't believe that both Jake and Tara would be making up what they saw and heard respectively.

He didn't want to say anything to Tara, but part of him wanted to go back to the Holden House without her and see if it happened again. The other part of him was scared to death to step foot back in that place. What if it was true and there was a ghost trying to hurt him?

He was deep in thought when Jake pulled up in front of the house. "You're here early."

Jake meandered up the stairs and plopped himself in a chair next to Ryan. He stretched out his legs on the railing and leaned his head back, closing his eyes. Ryan watched him, waiting for some form of communication from his friend.

A sigh escaped Jake's lips before he opened his eyes and glanced at Ryan. "Where is she?"

"Upstairs, in the shower last I knew."

Jake nodded. "I can't find out much about this Cecilia person. Not much in way of records way back to the start of the house. We need to find some 200-year-old person that can tell us what happened."

Ryan snorted. "Yeah, there is a load of 200 year olds sitting around just waiting to talk to us."

"I've got nothing for you, for Tara. She's gonna want to go back to that house again. Can you do that?"

Ryan sat forward. "What if we go back without her and do some searching?"

Jake dropped his feet to the floor. "You sure you want to do that? How's the headache this morning?"

"It's gone. Why not? Do you really believe some ghost was trying to hurt me yesterday?"

"Dude, absolutely. I know you don't believe in this stuff, but ghosts and spirits can really wreak havoc on a person they are angry with. I think we need to figure out why she is so angry with you."

The front door opened and out hobbled Tara. A sly grin on her face told Ryan that she had been listening to their conversation. "Whatcha thinking of doing today?"

"Not a thing. You're resting and I think I'll rest too. I'm wiped out."

Tara stared at Ryan. He knew by the look on her face he had used the wrong choice of wording. "...if you want?" he added. She rolled her eyes at him.

"I take it you couldn't find anything on our ghost, Jake?"

"Nada. There's no records dating back that long ago for when the house was built or who owned it...at least that I can find." Jake glanced between the two of them. "I think our best bet is to return to the house and do a full search top to bottom."

"I'm in," Tara announced.

Ryan put his head in his hands. "I feel like I'm being dragged into a nightmare that I can't escape."

"Dude, if you're scared you don't have to go."

Ryan looked up at Jake. "Really? You know I'm not scared and yet you feel the need to challenge my manhood over this?"

Laughter spilled out of Tara that caught both of the men off-guard. Neither of them had heard such a free laughter from her. She was holding her stomach, giggling nonstop.

"And you..." Ryan pointed at her, "are no better than he is."

"I'm ready when you are," Tara spoke between giggles.

"Fine. Give me a few minutes to change." Ryan grabbed his coffee mug and started inside.

Once Ryan was inside, Tara slid into the chair he had vacated and propped her foot up on the railing.

"How's the foot?"

"It's okay. Doesn't hurt too bad. I'm sorer from the use of the damn crutches than anything."

"In all seriousness, now that he's gone." Jake gestured with his head towards the house. "Are you really feeling up to going to the house, knowing that Cecilia could be after Ryan?"

"I think we need to find out who she is. I find it odd that she appeared so angry with him. Maybe he shouldn't go with us?"

"You know he's not going to let you out of his sight?"

Tara nodded. "I'm just as worried about him though."

"Well, I guess we better figure out this little mystery and put an end to all this." Jake stood up. "We know there is something about Ryan that is a trigger for her though. She didn't bother me at all when I was there by myself."

"So, what's the key? Maybe we should look into Ryan's ancestors." Tara drifted into her thoughts.

"What do you mean?" Jake leaned against the railing.

"Well, let's look at his ancestors and see if anyone in his family had any connection to the Holden House. Does he look like any of them? What was it about him that triggered the anger in Cecilia? I'm assuming he reminded her of someone she knew."

Jake nodded slowly. "That could work. It would keep Ryan out of the Holden House. And you off that foot."

Tara glared at him. "Now you're as bad as he is."

Jake held out his hand to her and pulled her to her feet. "I have to keep my friend happy too. Besides, you want that ankle to heal as soon as possible and staying off it would be a start."

Tara slipped her arm through his elbow and together they started inside. "Well, it will at least make Ryan happy to know we are staying here...how he will feel about digging into his past, I'm not sure."

Chapter Sixteen

RYAN HAD BEEN THRILLED ABOUT NOT GOING TO THE HOLDEN House again and with Tara on the couch with her ankle propped up, he was even happier to see her content to be resting. The part that didn't have him thrilled was Tara and Jake each on their laptops doing research on the Stafford family and his ancestors.

He didn't feel he had anything to hide, yet it was disconcerting to think they were scrutinizing every move his family had made over the past hundred years. He knew his grandfather had built a business from the ground up and had employed a lot of people in the past from this town. Everything Ryan remembered was that his grandfather was well-loved by everyone he had come in contact with.

"Man, your family has been loaded for centuries." Jake's random comment caught Ryan off-guard.

"Really? That's what you're focusing on."

"No, but it makes you uncomfortable, so it's worth bringing up." Jake chuckled to himself.

"Hey, this is interesting," Tara broke in. She patted the couch next to her for Ryan to sit down. "I'm looking at pictures instead of articles. Look at this picture. It could have been you in a previous life."

Ryan looked at the computer screen. There definitely was a close resemblance to the man in the picture and himself. "Who is it?"

Tara clicked on the picture. "Brandon Stafford." She continued to click on another link. "Doesn't look like he was very wealthy at all. In fact, it looks like he married for the simple fact to receive the dowry of his wife."

"Who was his wife?" Jake came around behind the couch to peer over her shoulder.

"It doesn't say. Simply that she died a year into their marriage and he inherited everything."

"Okay, but at least we have a name to go on. Maybe Cecilia herself can confirm if this was her husband." The excitement in Jake's voice grated on Ryan's nerves.

"Wait. I'm supposed to believe because I look like some long lost relative that is the reason this so-called ghost hates me?"

Tara laced her fingers with Ryan's. "So-called? Ry, come on. You know there is a lot of truth here with Cecilia and a reason that she doesn't like you."

"There has to be a different way to find out who this Brandon's wife was before going over there and confronting a ghost."

Jake made his way back around to the chair he had previously vacated. "What's going on, Ryan?"

"Well, it's not your family we're dissecting."

"Dude, we're not trying to dig up dirt on your family. We're simply trying to figure out why Cecilia is out to get you. I can say, I honestly don't care about what skeletons are in your closet."

"I don't either. Neither of our pasts matter, but I want to know what is going on." Tara's voice was soft and pleading.

Ryan knew there was nothing he could do or say that would deter these two amateur sleuths with a ghost story in their midst. He sighed. "Fine, but find out what you can online first before we have to go back to that house."

"I'm on it." Jake turned his attention back to his computer, oblivious to the other two in the room.

"Thank you. I know this isn't easy for you." Tara leaned her head on Ryan's shoulder.

"It's okay. Whatever we can do to get this behind us." He kissed her forehead gently, smiling as she snuggled closer.

They sat in silence with the only sound in the room coming from the typing as Jake searched for anything he could find on Ryan's family.

"Not much on this Brandon, but maybe we should start with an ancestry search going back from you, Ry."

Ryan shrugged. I know my immediate relatives.

Ryan paced the living room. Ever since agreeing to research his family ancestry, he was torn by what kind of skeletons were in his closet. What if Tara found something that made her decide she wanted nothing to do with him? He took four steps and stopped to look out the window. The whispering between Jake and Tara was grating on his nerves.

"Man, settle down," Jake's voice broke through his thoughts.

"What have you come up with?" He turned and

looked at Jake. His peripheral vision caught Tara watching him with a half-smile on her face.

"Nothing yet. It's not that simple." Jake rose and made his way to the coffee table. He picked up the pad of paper and handed it to Tara. "Let's write this all out. It will be easier to visualize the generations."

Tara nodded and started writing Ryan's name at the top. She gestured for him to come sit next to her.

"Did you have any siblings?" Her pen was posed next to Ryan's name ready to fill in the appropriate name.

Ryan glanced up at Jake. He didn't talk about his brother. He sighed and turned to Tara. "Geoffrey."

Tara wrote in the name and waited. "Where is he now?"

"Windhill Cemetery."

Tara reached for his hand. "I'm sorry, Ryan."

"He was two years younger than me." Ryan smiled. "That kid followed me everywhere, was really quite annoying as far as little brothers go. He died when he was seventeen."

"I'm so sorry, Ryan." Tara squeezed his hand.

"It's okay. It really has been a while now. He was such a happy kid, ready to be there to help anyone."

"What happened?" Tara's voice was a whisper.

"Leukemia." Ryan gestured to the paper, ready to move on. "Our parents were Timothy and Michelle."

Tara continued filling in the lineage.

"Grandparents were Marshall and Evelyn Stafford. I'm assuming we want to take this back up through my dad's side of the family since this Brandon Stafford was that side of the family?"

"I think that's a good place to start. If we hit a wall, we can add in your mom's side." Tara agreed.

"Beyond my great-grandparents, who were George and Bertha, I don't know." Ryan shrugged. "I'm realizing that doesn't take us back far enough, but that's all I know."

Jake spoke up. "We'll start with a Google search to see what comes up with your great-grandparents. If we don't get much, we'll visit some cemeteries and see what is written on their headstones for family members."

"It's going to take a while to figure some of this out." Tara doodled on the top of the paper.

"We don't have a deadline. We'll figure it out." Ryan stood. "But honestly, right now I'm starving. Food anyone?"

Jake nodded. He waited until Ryan left the room before sitting down next to Tara. "He's a bit sensitive about his brother. In fact, I haven't heard him talk about Geoff in years. He was devastated when he died."

"I'm sure. I can't imagine losing a sibling. But then again, I can't imagine having a sibling."

"You guys coming?" Ryan yelled from the foyer.

Tara and Jake joined him. "Where to?"

"Let's get out of here and go grab some pizza. Take our minds off this creepy ghost for a while." Ryan was antsy and the overwhelming feeling that the house was closing in on him was ready to make him crawl out of his skin.

The car was silent as they drove to the pizza place. Ryan tried to turn his mind off, but instead memories came flooding back of Geoffrey lying in bed at the end of his life. His body was an empty shell, withered away from the muscular young man he had become. His head was bald from the chemotherapy. Ryan had done everything he could to avoid seeing his brother. He had been a coward. Geoffrey had kept a smile on his face, regardless of being sick from the treatments; he had joked with Ryan, trying desperately to make Ryan feel comfortable with being with him. And Ryan had avoided him at all costs. Something Ryan would change in a heartbeat if he could just have a little more time with his brother.

The guilt had eaten away at him the past ten years that his brother had been gone. This was the reason he traveled so much and threw himself into his work. Geoffrey had died right here at Stafford House. The house he inherited from his grandfather. Ryan couldn't bear to be in the house, but somehow with Tara there with him, it was all bearable. Leave it to some old ghost torturing Tara to make him face his own past and the demons that resided there.

The trio entered the pizza parlor, making their way to a corner booth in the back. After agreeing on the kind of pizza and ordering, Tara glanced between Jake and Ryan.

"Is there any way we can be researching the Holden House at the same time?"

Jake nodded. "I ran into a dead end when looking for ownership of the house beyond Priscilla Holden who was the last person to own it. Older records had burnt in a fire that wiped out the courthouse years ago."

"Who owns it now?" Tara asked.

"That's it. According to Priscilla's will, it was left to her granddaughter, Anna Holden. However, they have been searching for her for the past few years and can't find her anywhere. It's like she fell off the face of the earth."

"Anna Holden? Anna owns the house now?" Ryan sat up straight.

Jake nodded.

The waitress set their pizza in the middle of the table. They all spoke a brief "Thanks" and dove into the pie.

Tara ate her piece before saying anything else. Once finished she reached for a second piece, but laid in it on her plate. "How do you know Anna wanted to be found? She was a kid."

"She was my best friend. I just know," Ryan snapped.

"Ry..." Jake broke in.

"I know, I'm sorry. I just know Anna would have wanted to stay in touch."

"Okay, but you don't know why her parents moved her so quickly. Maybe there was a reason for the secretiveness." Tara bit into her pizza.

Ryan chewed thoughtfully, mulling over Tara's comments. He had never thought about that. He knew for years his grandfather had been trying to locate them and never could. He had assumed it was because Ryan was lost without Anna, but maybe there was another reason.

"Maybe we need to do Anna's genealogy," Jake joked.

"That's not a bad idea." Ryan agreed.

"I was kidding and you're only agreeing because you don't want to discuss your family," Jake pointed out.

Ryan nodded. "In part, yes, but on the other hand it may give us some insight on how to find out who owned the house. If we are going to be doing these family trees, wouldn't it be just as easy to research both families at the same time?"

Tara broken in. "It would probably work, especially if the families were both originally from here and then we would be at a place where we would have to be doing research on both of them." Tara pulled a notebook from her purse. "I'll start separate pages for each family."

Jake laughed. "There's Nancy Drew, ready to solve the mystery."

"You won't be laughing when I break the case," Tara retorted.

They ate in silence until the pie was gone and they each sat back distracted by their own thoughts.

"Where do we go from here?" Ryan broke the silence.

Jake glanced between him and Tara. "My guess is we do an Internet search and see what we come up with. We don't have to do this all tonight, you know?"

Ryan nodded. He threw down money on the table to cover the bill and stood.

"Guess you're ready to go?" Tara stood.

"Sorry. Am I rushing you guys?"

Tara laughed. "No. You're just lost in your own thoughts apparently. I get it, but don't shut us out if it is something that could help us."

———

Tara fell into bed, hoping the fact that she was exhausted would help her go right into a dreamless sleep. She needed a peaceful night. She had spent too many nights of late trying to stay awake to avoid the dreams of her grandmother and whoever's memories flooded her.

She tossed and turned, struggling to go to sleep and yet keep her mind clear. Every time she turned over, her mind would drift to her grandmother. A faceless voice that was calming, yet torturing her with these instructions that Tara had no idea what they meant. She dozed off to a fitful sleep.

Tara, you must let him in. Don't fight it.

Tara sat up in bed. She was drenched in sweat once

more. This was getting old fast. She threw back the covers and reached for her sweatshirt. She pulled it on over her tank top as she slipped her feet into a pair of slippers. She grabbed her laptop and started downstairs. Coffee. That would help. Armed with coffee and her laptop, she figured she could continue the searched for Ryan's relatives, or maybe *Ryan's* Anna's family.

Chapter Seventeen

RYAN HAD BEEN HARD-PRESSED TO FALL ASLEEP. DIGGING INTO his past wasn't sitting well with him. He had pushed away the memories of Geoff for years, and now he was having to relive them. Every time he closed his eyes, he saw his brother lying in that damn hospital bed, thin as a rail. He could no longer picture his brother as healthy. He couldn't remember what Geoff looked like before the leukemia claimed him.

Ryan suppressed the tears as long as he could. With a heartbroken sob, he allowed the tears to overtake him. It had been years since he had cried for his brother, for the missed time they had, for the brotherly advice Ryan would never receive or give. Sometimes it was the things that he had never had with his brother that Ryan missed the most. There was an unspoken pain that no one could understand because he wasn't quite sure what it was he was missing out on.

Ryan immersed himself in his pain and allowed his body to cleanse itself with the tears. After he was done, he got up and jumped in the shower. Although it was early morning hours and he doubted anyone was awake, he felt the need to shower and start the day. His mind was too jumbled to go back to sleep. After showering, he crept down the stairs hoping Tara was sleeping. He smelled the coffee before he got to the kitchen and realized all his efforts to be quiet were for naught. Entering the kitchen, he saw Tara hunched over her computer, coffee cup in hand.

"Did you make enough for me?"

Tara jumped and whirled in her chair to face him. "What are you doing up? Did I wake you?"

He shook his head. "No, you didn't wake me. Couldn't sleep."

She pointed to the coffee pot. "There is more than enough for you."

Ryan doctored up his coffee and joined her at the table. "What are you working on?"

He watched her as guilt flitted across her face. "Genealogy for the Stafford family."

He laughed. "It's okay. I knew you were going to keep digging." He cleared his throat as he sat back. "I want to apologize for earlier. I know I got a bit snippy when you started asking questions. I haven't talked about Geoff in a long time and I guess I wasn't sure I wanted to open those memories back up."

"I had no idea. I'm sorry." Tara dropped her eyes. "I didn't mean to cause you pain, Ryan."

"You didn't." Ryan pulled his chair from across the table to next to Tara's. "What did you find?"

Tara pushed the computer toward Ryan so he could see it clearer. "Beyond your great-grandparents, I haven't found much. I think I need to join one of those genealogy sites so I can have access to more information."

"You have to pay for those sites?"

Tara nodded. "But worth it, especially if we are going to look at Anna's family tree also. I can always cancel it when we are done. I think there is an option to pay for it monthly."

"Let me pay for it. After all, it is my family that you are researching."

Tara started shaking her head no, but seemed to be thinking better of it before giving in.

Ryan sat back and watched as she went to a site and created an account. There was a seven-day trial period so they started that option and opened the research. Tara started with doing a search for Timothy and Michelle Stafford, Ryan's parents. As predicted, and it matched the information Tara already had, Marshall and Evelyn came up as Timothy's parents. Ryan nodded and leaned closer to Tara. "This is really fascinating the way you can find people here. How do they pull all this up?"

"It comes from censuses, birth and death records, military records. Any type of public record really. As it goes back further in time, it's hard because a lot of those records aren't digitized and so sometimes it takes longer. Another hint came up relating to Marshall Stafford. His sisters, Sonia and Ava, who were both older linking them to their parents, George and Bertha. Impossible to think that in just a few short keystrokes, Ryan was looking at relatives that went back over 90 years since he had been born.

They seemed to be at a standstill and Ryan glanced at the clock. It was *only* 5 a.m. It seemed like they had been up for hours, or at least he had been. He couldn't imagine what time Tara had gotten up. "Hungry?"

Tara nodded as she continued to look at hints that

popped up. He left her at it and went to the fridge. As he pulled out eggs, cheese, Canadian bacon, mushrooms, and fresh spinach, he hummed softly. He whipped together omelets for them and put some English muffins into the toaster.

When everything was ready, he slid the plate of food in front of Tara and sat down next to her. He took in the tree that had blossomed on her computer with all the matches she had been able to pull together for Ryan's family. Ryan never knew his ancestors beyond his great-grandparents, having only heard of their names being mentioned. He had known his grandparents, but it was neat to see the aunts and uncles, and even great aunts that he had never known add branches to the tree.

They ate in silence and after both had had their fill, Tara pulled the computer closer to her again. "Do you think we should try and do Anna's?"

Ryan nodded. "We can try. I don't remember her parents' names, but we did hear that Priscilla was the name of her grandmother according to Jake and the will that they came across.

Tara plugged in Anna Holden and nothing came up. She then went to Priscilla Holden and still nothing came up. They seemed to hit a brick wall and Tara looked at Ryan. "What if we are going about this wrong?"

"What do you mean?"

Tara stared at the computer. "What if it isn't the genealogy that we really need to work on, but what if it is the owner of the house. You say this house has been in your family since it was built. What if the Holden House has the same lineage? Maybe we can find Anna's family that way."

Ryan nodded. "It's worth a shot, but that would

require us to wait until normal work hours to go to the Town Hall to see the tax maps."

Tara agreed. "It's much easier if we can just work in the middle of the night."

"Maybe it would be much better if we could just actually sleep." Ryan stood and reached for her hand. "Let's lay down on the couch and just talk. Maybe you can get some sleep."

"Maybe you can get some sleep," Tara countered, but grabbed his hand and stood up. They settled into the couch, Ryan spooning Tara and holding her close.

"What time did you get up?"

Tara closed her eyes. "I'm not sure. I wouldn't have said it was that much before you, but I had finished a full cup of coffee before you came down and I did get lost in the research a bit. Maybe an hour."

Ryan nodded. He felt her breathing change as she drifted away in his arms. He closed his eyes and held her tight. For once, his mind was clear from ghosts, ones unknown and ones known.

Chapter Eighteen

Tara woke to the front door opening. She laid still and listened to footsteps come across the foyer into the living room. She glanced up over the couch to see Jake tiptoeing in.

"I'm awake."

Jake pointed to Ryan. "Sleeping beauty isn't though."

"We were up late, or up early this morning doing research." Tara moved quietly to get off the couch, trying not to wake Ryan. "Want some coffee?"

"Sure."

Jake followed Tara to the kitchen where she made a fresh pot of coffee. She pointed to her notes by the computer. "We made some progress on the Stafford tree, but we think it might be easier to look for ownership of the Holden House back through the years. What do you think?"

Jake nodded. "Do you think this Cecilia is a Holden?"

"We don't know really. We know she obviously doesn't like at least one of the Stafford men, one that looks like Ryan."

She poured them each a mug of coffee and placed them on the kitchen. She fetched creamer and sugar, delivering them to Jake before sitting down. "Do you think she is a Holden or is it possible that house wasn't originally from the Holden family?"

Tara shrugged. "I don't know. I love the thought of tracing the ancestry back and finding out more about it. I'm drawn to that house and for whatever reason, my grandmother is leading me there."

"Do you remember your grandmother? I mean, did you know her personally?" Jake asked.

"I remember talking to her on the phone some when I was little. She died when I was in my teens. I don't remember seeing her, just the phone calls. There were very little pictures in my house growing up. I have some old school pictures from when I was a kid and into high school, but really nothing prior to age ten. I don't remember it, but my parents told me we had a house fire and everything was destroyed. I had been trapped in the fire, and according to them, I had been injured bad and that I had lost my memories."

Jake watched her. "You don't remember anything from your childhood really?"

"Not younger than ten. It's like my life just started at that age. We were in a new house and that's where my memories appear to start. I don't remember the house fire at all."

"Amnesia happens, but doesn't it usually come back at some point?"

Tara shrugged. "I don't know. I never really questioned it."

They both turned as Ryan walked into the kitchen.

"You know you are going to make yourself sick with the amount of coffee you drink."

Tara stuck out her tongue at him. "Do you want a cup?"

Ryan went to the fridge and pulled out a bottled water. "I think I'll hydrate instead."

"Don't expect me to give up my one vice," Tara said.

Jake laughed. "I hardly think coffee is your one vice."

Tara winked. "I'll never tell."

Tara could feel Ryan's eyes on her and she glanced at him and smiled. She knew he seemed a bit tense whenever Jake was around and she wondered if he was feeling possessive. She hoped not because she didn't do well with people thinking they owned her. She drained her coffee and stood. "I'll let you two chat. I'm going to go grab a shower so we can get to the Town Hall when it opens."

As she left the kitchen, she could hear Ryan moving over to the table. She didn't want to be the cause of tension between the two friends and she feared that somehow, she would get caught in something she didn't want to be a part of.

She stood under the hot water as it rained over her. She allowed herself the moment to relax and just enjoy the heat. She closed her eyes to release the strain of the chaos. *You need him.* The words from her grandmother broke through and Tara nodded. She knew instinctively her grandmother was talking about Ryan. But was Ryan the one she had been told to find? Were they one in the same or was there someone else that her grandmother wanted her to find? Tara didn't know what she should be doing next, but she willed her grandmother to lead her forward.

Telling Jake about her lack of childhood memories seemed to shake Tara. She suddenly couldn't figure out why she had no memories and if it was amnesia, why hadn't the memories come back? She made a mental note to talk to her childhood doctor about it. Maybe a conversation with him would fill in the blanks. Once again, she had a strong yearning for her parents to still be alive so she could talk to them about all this.

She towel-dried and after getting dressed, sat cross-legged on her bed. She pulled her phone to her and dialed the doctor's office. She hadn't spoken to the doctor in a few years. She had an aversion for some reason to go to the doctor's office and only went if she was truly sick. After leaving a message for Dr. Everson to call her back, she hung up and laid back against her pillows. She was exhausted and yet her mind ran constantly. She closed her eyes and tried to picture her grandmother. She could hear her voice just like she did on the phone when she was a kid, but had she truly never seen her grandmother?

Her laptop was downstairs, so she picked up her phone and googled for articles on fires at her childhood home. Nothing came up. She then googled Holden scandal and still nothing came up. She tried Stafford scandal, and a small article popped up mentioning a man named David Holden embezzling money from Stafford Enterprises a couple of decades ago, but other than that, there were no other articles and the whole *embezzling scandal* just seemed to disappear. The name David Holden meant nothing to her.

Ryan's voice broke through her thoughts, "Tara, you ready?"

She grabbed her phone and headed for the stairs. It was time to go digging for answers.

Chapter Nineteen

THE TRIO WALKED INTO THE TOWN HALL AND ASKED FOR LAND ownership maps for the area where the Holden House stood. The clerk frowned at them before going into the back office to speak with someone. A young man came out.

"Can I help you?"

Ryan stepped forward. "We are looking to research the ownership of the land where the Holden House stands."

"Can I ask why?"

Jake stepped forward, showing his private investigation license. "I'm working on behalf of a family member and they are looking to establish the genealogy of the property. Is there a problem? They are public records, are they not?"

The man nodded. "No problem. It's just been a long time since someone has wanted to see those records. In fact, it is on record that they have been moved to our archive office."

"Is that common to move records?" Jake asked.

"Not really, but apparently, it was requested that they be moved. I have no idea who; it was long before I started here. I can request them, but it will take a few days."

They thanked the man and put in the request. Jake signed the request, simply putting down *confidential* in the *requested by* line. As they walked down the sidewalk, Tara between the two men, she suddenly stopped. "Does it seem odd that those records have been moved? Was someone trying to hide something?"

Jake shrugged. "It could simply be because they couldn't find the owners. I would have to research to see how long ownership can be held if an heir cannot be found. I would assume the state would take over the deed."

"How long do they wait before they take it over? You said they were searching for this Anna Holden? How long before she forfeits it?" Tara asked.

"I don't know." Jake frowned. "I'll see if I can get some information on that."

Tara glanced at Ryan. "You haven't said much."

Ryan whispered. "I just wonder where she is and if she is okay."

"We'll get answers." Tara reached for his hand and squeezed. "We'll find out what happened to her."

Ryan just nodded and looked at Jake. Tara saw the look that passed between them. She knew they had known each other long enough to know what each other's looks meant. She felt a bit left out, but didn't say a word. Obviously, this Anna was important to Ryan, even if he hadn't seen her in years. Was it just that he needed closure, or was there more there?

"I'm going to head to the Holden House. I want to

look around some more," Tara said, bringing the other two to an abrupt stop.

"Now?" Ryan asked.

She nodded. "It's okay if you don't want to go. I'll be careful."

Both spoke at once. "You're not going alone."

Her lips twitched as she suppressed a knowing smile. She changed their course as the two men followed behind her. They approached from the driveway and Tara stopped at the front of the house. She could picture the grand view it must have made in its heyday. Although the paint was peeling and it was falling down from lack of maintenance, Tara could see the status this house would have evoked in the town.

She glanced back at Ryan and Jake, who still had yet to say a word and she started around the back to the kitchen entrance. As they entered the building, Tara stopped and listened. It was silent, staleness in the air, which made her pause. It was like they were alone in the house. She moved through the house until she got to the stairway, and started climbing to the second floor. They guys were behind her, and when she glanced back she saw that Ryan had dropped back behind Jake.

They reached the second floor without incident and Tara turned toward Ryan. "You okay?"

"I'm good."

They moved forward and Tara stopped at the door where Jake had seen Cecilia before. The trio moved into the room and Tara walked around the edges of the room, stopping at the window to look out. The window over-looked the backyard. The yard from this view needed a good weeding out and cutting back of dead flowers and shrubs. This would have been a beautiful view back when it was first built. Tara could see remnants of flower beds that would have been bursting with color.

A cool breeze brushed past Tara's face and she turned toward the center of the room. Ryan and Jake had moved into the next room, closet area, when suddenly the door between them shut with a force.

Ryan started banging on the door. "Tara, are you okay?"

"I'm good. Can you open it?" Tara had tried turning the knob, but it appeared to be locked and there was no key in the keyhole.

"It's locked," Ryan answered.

The cool breeze swirled around Tara and she stepped back away from the door. It kept pulling her toward the main door in the room. "I'll be right back," she said as she allowed herself to be pulled from the room.

"Tara, stay here with us," Jake yelled.

"It's okay. Trust me," Tara answered. Getting to the top of the stairs, the cool breeze dissipated and Tara paused. "Cecilia, are you here?"

A shimmer at the bottom of the stairs caught Tara's eyes and she squinted to see what it was. A blueish hue seemed to float down the hallway. She felt she was being beckoned. Although questioning her judgment at following it, she hurried down the stairs and followed the blur. She had no doubt it was Cecilia, who wanted to show her something. Tara almost had to run to keep up with the hue. Suddenly it disappeared next to a door to her right. Tara opened the door into what looked like a study. There were bookcases lining a wall and a heavy desk stood in the middle of the room. Behind the layers of filth on top of it, the wood was scarred with scratches, but at one time would have stood in glory in this room.

A cool gentle breeze once more settled around Tara and she turned. She did not see the blue hue, but was pulled toward the bookcases. Many of the shelves were empty now, but there were a few tomes scattered about on some of the shelves. A mark in the dust started showing and Tara looked closer. It was like a finger was moving along the shelf and stopped at the wall. Tara frowned. She felt a push toward the wall and Tara reached for the wall to grab it before she fell into it. As she grabbed just above where the mark had been made in the dust, she felt a click under her finger. She ran her finger over the spot again and could feel a small indentation. She pushed a little bit and the bookcase fell back, opening into the wall itself.

Tara almost rubbed her hands together in anticipation of this hidden area. "Cecilia, what is this? I should get the boys."

A cold blast hit her. *Okay, no guys will come,* she thought and the air warmed slightly. She needed to follow Cecilia into this passageway and she was a bit unsure about it. She grabbed her phone from her back pocket and clicked on the flashlight app to illuminate the path. She stepped forward slowly, putting one foot in front of the other with a slight hesitation. The corridor didn't look like it went far. A dead end, maybe. Once inside, Tara hesitated, not wanting the door to shut behind her and yet another cool breeze pushed her further in.

Thankfully Cecilia left the door open and Tara kept going. She had gone about a few feet when there seemed to be a solid wall in front of her. She turned slowly and held her flashlight up, looking at every inch of the wall on either side of her. "Cecilia, what is it I need to see?"

As Tara turned back toward the door where she had entered, her light caught a small shelf to the side built into the wall behind the door as it stood open. She moved toward it and pulled the door to a half open position. She kept it open just enough so she could reach behind it to the shelf. It was hardly a shelf she realized, but more of a crevice in which something was wedged.

Take it. It was a command from a female voice. Definitely not her grandmother's, so must be Cecilia, Tara thought.

She pulled the soft package from the hiding place. It was wrapped in a linen wrap. Tara stepped back into the study and laid it on the desk. She shut her phone off and jumped as the bookcase slammed back into place. The air was still once more and she knew instinctively that Cecilia was gone. She heard a door open upstairs and both Jake and Ryan calling her name as they charged down the stairs.

"I'm in here," she yelled. She was staring at the package when they both came running down the hall and into the study.

"What happened?" Ryan demanded.

"I was shown a secret passage and found this," Tara said and pointed.

Jake looked around the room. "Where was the passage?"

Tara turned toward the bookcase and noticed there was no mark in the dust any longer. She shrugged. "Somewhere in the bookcase. I don't know now. She closed it back up once I came back out here."

"You went into a secret passage by yourself knowing we were locked upstairs?" Ryan asked.

"It was what she wanted. I think she locked you guys

up there because she didn't want you to know about the passage."

Ryan shook his head. "Sounds like she's kind of biased against me and you, Jake." He didn't sound upset, more in awe at how things seemed to be going.

Tara opened the linen and inside found a soft leather cover around paper. A diary. "We need to take this home and read it." She closed her eyes. *Is that okay, Cecilia, to take it with us?* A soft breeze slid through the ends of her hair, warm-like fingers being run through her hair. Tara took that as a yes.

Chapter Twenty

THEY ARRIVED BACK AT RYAN'S HOUSE AND CROWDED ONTO THE living room couch with Tara in the middle and Ryan and Jake flanking her. She opened the book slowly. The pages were old and yellowed. She wondered just how old this diary was and if no one else had ever found it.

There were no dates, but the first page had flowers drawn all around the edges of the page. *Today is the day! My wedding day. I cannot believe it is finally here. Momma and Daddy have been tirelessly preparing for this day. Momma made my trousseau and it is lovely. I hope Brandon is as excited as I am to start this life together. It has been a short courtship, but daddy assures me that this is the right man for me and our family. Brandon wants to work with daddy and as daddy says, he good promise. I don't care about any of that. Daddy has gifted us the Holden House for our wedding. Tonight I will start my life there. To think I have my own house to run. Momma has prepared me for this, though she hadn't said much about the wedding night. I'm nervous to think of my husband and my duties for him tonight. Momma says to just be relaxed and Brandon will help me understand what needs to be done.*

Tara looked back and forth from Jake to Ryan. They had sat back on the couch listening to her as she read it. Cecilia was married to Brandon. She jumped up and ran to grab her notebook. She wrote down Brandon. She assumed he must have been a Stafford, but they weren't sure yet. She came back to the living room. She sank onto the carpet, facing Ryan and Jake, and turned the page of the diary.

The wedding was beautiful. I wasn't sure about the wedding night, and I guess it was okay. Momma did not prepare me for what Brandon would want from me. I was a bit shocked to say the least when I finally understood what my duty was to be. He wasn't impatient with me, but he wasn't very patient either. I hope next time will be better. I had thought we were to go off for a few days for a honeymoon, but Brandon told me at breakfast that he didn't have time for a honeymoon. Instead he is going to be leaving for a business trip and I will be staying here. I hope this isn't what our marriage will be like. Momma and Daddy's marriage seems so different. Maybe it was the same as this in their early years. I will need to ask Momma about it.

There were a few doodles on the page, but the flowers were gone.

In the short span of one night, Tara could feel the heartbreak that Cecilia had endured so quickly in her marriage. No wonder this woman doesn't like the Stafford men. Tara was almost afraid to read any further, afraid that she would see more heartache and no happiness from this woman.

"Doesn't sound like a very loving start to a marriage," Jake mused out loud.

"Very disappointing to her, I would imagine." Ryan pointed to the diary. "Can we skip ahead a bit?"

Tara shrugged. "You don't want to hear every day?"

Ryan laughed. "By all means, if that is what you want to do. I was just hoping to jump to something that would actually give us some answers."

"I can always read the gaps later without you." She smirked, but skipped ahead and found a few entries near the end. Going back about four days before the last entry, she started reading.

It's been almost a year since Brandon and I got married and he has totally destroyed my love for him. He never loved me. He only wanted this house. I tried to talk to daddy about it, but daddy said marriage is always a business deal. And according to him, women have no say in business deals. Blast them all. I tried to talk to Momma, but she just tells me that I expect too much from things and that I need to be happy with what I have. I'm not happy. I wanted a marriage of love and wanted to start a family. Instead, apparently Brandon will be having a family with his mistress and not me. He has not come to my bed in months. He doesn't even try to hide that he has a mistress. It's humiliating for me. The staff all know and won't even treat me like I have any authority of them. I don't. Brandon has made sure to undermine me in all I have tried to do with the staff. They only respect him and have made it quite clear they will not work for me. When he is not home, I cannot even get them to bring me tea. Alas, I don't even feel comfortable going to my own kitchen to fix it myself.

Tara sighed. "She's so lonely."

Jake and Ryan didn't say anything. Tara turned to the last entry. "Last one."

This is it. Our one year anniversary. How fitting that it will all end today. I went into town today and came face to face with HER and her belly that was a slap in the face to me. She is due very soon and I cannot believe she has not started her confinement yet. It was all I could do to look her in the eyes and just walk by. She seemed surprised to see me. I can only imagine what Brandon has told her. I'm twenty-five years old and my life is over. I hope that when he comes home and sees me, he will want to make amends.

"That's it," Tara said. "What do you think happened?"

"It must have been the day she died. But how did she die?" Ryan mused.

Jake stood and started pacing around the room. "We know she married Brandon and I assume from her lack of warm feelings for Ryan that Brandon was a Stafford. What I don't understand though, why is it still called Holden House if it was a wedding present to them. Was Cecilia a Holden?"

"This doesn't give us many answers, other than we know she married and died on their one-year anniversary and her husband, Brandon, was an obvious dickhead," Tara said.

Ryan laughed. "Those damn Stafford men." He then sobered. "I don't remember ever hearing his name. I wonder if there are any records in the attic that my grandfather would have kept?"

Tara jumped up. "Let's go see."

Tara and Jake followed Ryan upstairs. At the end of the hall on the second floor was a doorway. Ryan pulled it open to reveal a narrow flight of stairs that led to the attic. "Careful on these. They are steep and narrow."

He flicked on the light switch on the wall as they climbed up the stairs. The attic space was huge compared to what Tara was expecting. There was furniture covered with dust clothes and old steam trunks over to one side.

Ryan headed for an old wooden filing cabinet on the other side of the attic. He flipped on another light as he went, one of those lights that really was just a light bulb with a chain hanging down, but it lit up the other end of the attic. More furniture covered as well. Ryan pulled open the top drawer and pulled out a couple of small cedar boxes. He set them on one of the pieces of furniture, stirring up a puff of dust. Opening the box, he pulled out some papers and started sifting through them.

Tara poked around the desk, opening drawers, and looking through them. Nothing seemed to be out of the ordinary. She looked up at Jake who was looking through the steamer trunks. He glanced up at Tara. "Just a bunch of old clothes...cool looking, very old."

Tara walked over to Ryan. "What is all this?"

"Mostly old business papers, but interesting is a copy of a note to the Town Hall, asking that the records for Holden House be archived. Why would my grandfather be the one that asked for the records to be archived?" Jake and Tara crowded around Ryan to see what he was talking about.

"He must have known more about the Holden House than you thought," Tara murmured.

Ryan placed the papers back in the box and closed it. "Let's call it a day."

The tone in his voice left no doubt that he didn't want to know anything more today. Jake and Tara nodded. Once downstairs, Tara watched Ryan carefully. He was keeping his face neutral, but his stance was one of being on edge. Tara wished she knew what to say to him to ease his mind. Was he thinking of Anna and if his grandfather had known where Anna and her family had gone? Was he instrumental in keeping them apart?

"I'm going for a walk," Ryan said softly as he headed for the front door. Tara and Jake stayed in the living room.

Once the door shut, Tara turned to Jake. "He's thinking of Anna, isn't he?"

Jake nodded. "I imagine it's a shock to know his grandfather was involved. There definitely is more to this story than Ryan may want to find out."

"What can we do?"

Jake shrugged. "Not sure right now. Keep focusing in on Cecilia. I'll touch base with Ry about Anna."

Tara nodded. She couldn't help but feel she was being left out of that conversation on purpose, but she wasn't about to push it. She pulled Cecilia's diary to her and opened it once more. She opened it more towards the middle hoping it was about halfway into the year of Cecilia's marriage.

Today was not a fun day for me. We had an argument and Brandon told me I was naïve to think that he married me because he actually cared for me. He laughed at me and told me about his mistress. He also informed me he would no longer be needing me to do my 'duties' and assured me that there would be no children born into this marriage. I was heartbroken and he just seemed to laugh harder at my tears. I hate this wretched man...hate him with all my being.

Tara swallowed hard. Her heart broke for Cecilia and the cruelty that Brandon had inflicted on her. Tara couldn't imagine being in a loveless marriage, especially if you thought there had been love. Apparently Cecilia had been a bit naïve, but why didn't her mother prepare her better for how men were in the 1800s. Tara sighed. She often wondered as she got older, if she would find that one person who she would love forever and that would love her forever. She certainly wasn't old by any

stretch as she was just coming to her twenty-fifth birthday, but she still hated the thought that she would end
up alone. And every time she thought of her birthday,
beyond the thought of being alone, there was this
impending dread that she couldn't put her finger on.

Chapter Twenty-One

Ryan walked for what seemed like forever, lost in thought. Hands in his pockets, watching his feet as he moved along, his thoughts churned. Cecilia, his grandfather, ancestors...none of it made sense to him, yet this web of lies that seem to enfold his family had landed him right in the middle of the web. He was caught. He stopped and looked up. He was standing in front of the Holden House. He had been drawn here, but he couldn't pinpoint why. There was no way he was going in that house knowing that Cecilia hated him.

Cecilia. Did he truly believe in ghosts suddenly? He couldn't deny the things that had happened while he was in the house...he witnessed it. He experienced her anger directed at him and yet there was a tiny part within him that was screaming it wasn't true. Had his grandfather believed in ghosts? Did he know what had happened here? There were so many unanswered questions. And then there was Anna. Ryan stepped up on the first step of the veranda and sat down. He felt safe outside of the house. Maybe it was just hopeful thinking that the ghost couldn't reach him out here.

This place held memories of Anna, and yet there was more to it. He pulled out his phone. *Meet me at the Holden House. Alone.* He sent the text and sat back. He jumped when his phone vibrated with a text.

On my way. You ok?

I'm fine, Ryan responded. This place at one point must have been the talk of the town. The house was huge for this area. Ryan had always thought that the Stafford House was the mansion of the town and he had always just thought of this house as the house where the eccentric lady lived. But taking in the yard and exterior of this place, Ryan realized the extravagance of it, especially for the time period it was built in. The question was why was Tara so drawn to this place?

He stood as a car drove up. Jake got out of the car and walked to the front of it. He leaned against it and waited.

"I know," Ryan stated.

Jake chuckled. "You know what? That you are out of your mind coming here by yourself, or that you are out of your mind because you are freaking out over your family history?"

"Both."

"Dude, what's going on?"

Ryan shook his head and leaned on the car next to Jake. They both stared at the house in front of them. "I have this gut feeling that there is going to be stuff coming out that I don't know and not sure I want to know."

"We all have skeletons in our closets." Jake glanced at him. "What do we know?"

"I know my grandfather knew something about Anna and her family. I just don't know what that is yet."

"How do you know that?" Jake asked.

"The papers in the attic. My grandfather was the one that requested the records be archived. Why?"

"Could be any number of reasons? He was a lawyer. Did he work for the Holden family?"

Ryan's lips pressed together. "If he was there, there could be a lot more that we don't know."

"Would any of his old business records still be upstairs?"

Ryan nodded absently. "Yes, there are boxes of his business records. I'm just not sure I want to explore all that with Tara around."

"You think that's fair to her?"

"It's not about being fair. It's about me wanting to know my family secrets before I share them with others." Ryan stood up straight, sighing. "Let's go back to the house. I'll search the attic. You and Tara can work on the Holden aspect of it and Anna's family tree."

Chapter Twenty-Two

THE VOICE TAUNTED TARA AS SHE TOSSED AND TURNED. THE restlessness of her night had taken her down a dark path. Her grandmother's voice came calling out for her, but she couldn't see her. The darkness surrounded her and closed in. Tara shivered and wrapped her arms around herself. Her grandmother's voice was distressed and Tara searched for her. There were flashes of lights and in that moment, Tara thought she could see someone, but it wasn't her grandmother.

Come to me, the strange female voice called to her. Tara felt a pull. She stood and pulled on her sneakers that had been beside the bed. She walked down the stairs, her hand gliding down the banister. She opened the door and walked out into the cool night air. The voice was insistent and determined for her to move along, and Tara quickened her pace. Her grandmother's voice again called her name and was quickly hushed by the other female voice. Where were they taking her? Tara moved in a haze, sleep still holding firm to her, as she walked down the sidewalk until she got to the shortcut to Holden House. She instinctively moved along the path, her feet avoiding anything in her way. The voice urged her on and Tara quickened her pace to almost a jog. Tara skirted the hole in the ground that she and Ryan had come across before, and she slowed and looked into it. A small girl looked up at her and called out for help. Tara stopped and peered into the dark.

Hurry! You don't have much time, the voice broke through Tara's foggy mind and she turned and continued walking towards the shadow of a house through the trees. Branches pulled at her hair as she moved among the trees, walking faster and faster as she came closer to the house. The house stared down at her when she reached the clearing and Tara stopped short. The house had a personality and Tara could see it clearly at the moment. A personality that was filled with hate and anger.

Quick, upstairs. Tara felt a cold breeze push her towards the house. Tara mentally searched for her grandmother. Where was she? Why couldn't she hear her anymore?

She's fine, the voice whispered in her ear.

She was halfway up the stairs when her grandmother's voice came to her. *Be careful, dear. Don't let her fool you.* Tara stopped on the stairway and looked around. The house was bright, like it was the middle of summer and the sun was flooding the windows. She peered into the dark recesses of the hallway above her. There didn't seem to be much light up there, but she continued up the stairs, anyway. She shivered as she reached the hallway.

Come with me, the voice was beside her and Tara turned her head to see a young woman dressed in blue walk beside her. Her arm chilled as the girl intertwined their arms to move to the back of the hallway.

"Who are you?" Tara asked.

You know who I am.

"Cecilia?"

The girl's giggle washed over Tara and she shivered. "Where are we going?"

I want you to see my playmate. The girl let go of Tara's arm and ran ahead to a room at the end of the hall. Tara twisted the door handle, but it didn't budge against the lock. "Wait, Cecilia."

She could hear Cecilia in the room laughing and yet there seemed to be some crying as well. Tara struggled with the door. A warm breeze enveloped her and she could hear her grandmother. *Come, dear. You don't want to go in there.* Tara turned suddenly, headed back down the stairs and back to Stafford House. She made her way past the hole again, and it was empty this time. She stared for a moment before she continued on. Suddenly, Tara felt chilled and ran her hands over her arms. She was cold and wet. She blinked her eyes and looked around as she found herself standing at the edge of the woods, looking out at the sidewalk. She started jogging, speeding up to a full run to get back to the warmth of the house and see Ryan and Jake.

She couldn't tell when she bounded up the porch steps if she was crying or if it was just the rain streaming down her face. The front door was open and she stopped on the porch, bent over, heaving for breath. Her wet clothes clung to her as she shivered—from the rain and the shock of realizing she had been sleepwalking. She never remembered doing that before, but she knew without a doubt where she had been. She slipped off her shoes and tiptoed into the house. She shut the door quietly behind her and scurried across the foyer into the kitchen. She grabbed a tea towel and started drying her hair and wiping herself down. She shivered again and decided a hot shower was exactly what she needed. She started up the stairs and there stood Ryan at the top.

"Are you okay? Where have you been?" He rapid fired questions at her as he hurried to her side.

"Apparently, I was sleepwalking and got caught in the rain." Tara tried to brush it off, but she was shivering uncontrollably now, and Ryan pulled him to her. He scooped her up and went to the bathroom where she sat her down gently on the counter. He turned on the shower full blast and monitored the temperature.

"Take a shower. I'll make coffee." Ryan was out the door before she could say a word. She stripped off her wet clothes, leaving them in a heap on the floor. She stepped into the hot water and just stopped there with her eyes closed as the water washed the chill away. As she warmed, she reached for the shampoo and washed her hair. As she rinsed her hair, her mind raced with thoughts of why Cecilia would call her to the house. And what was behind that door at the end of the room? There was so much going on that Tara's mind started aching with the tax of trying to keep up with the thoughts. And where was her grandmother? Why had she allowed it and didn't intervene until she couldn't open the door?

Tara shut the water off and reached for a towel. She dried off and dressed in warm sweatpants and a sweat-shirt. She combed through her wet hair and shook it out with her fingers. The curls would come and she didn't care at this moment. She wanted something hot to drink and to feel Ryan's arms around her.

Ryan and Jake were both in the kitchen when Tara got downstairs. Neither of them said a word. Jake stood and pulled out a chair for her while Ryan poured her a mug of coffee. Both of the men already had a cup in front of them. Tara smiled at Jake as she sank into the chair and curled her legs up underneath her. Ryan handed her the mug and both of the men sat down...and waited.

Tara took her time drinking the coffee, letting the warmness move through her body until she felt sufficiently armed enough to speak. "Jake, why are you up?"

He raised an eyebrow at her. "Why? Because I'm worried about you. Ryan doesn't have the monopoly on that."

Tara gave him a small smile. "I'm fine."

Ryan sighed. "What happened? Have you always sleepwalked?"

She shook her head. "Not that I remember." She took another sip. "It was the strangest thing. I remember what happened. I heard Cecilia calling to me, and I could hear my grandmother. There was this need...this pull...that I had to get there in a hurry. I must have put on my sneakers and just gone. The door was open when I got back, so I must not have shut it." She turned to Ryan. "I'm sorry."

Ryan reached for her hand. "Nothing to be sorry about. I'm just glad you are okay."

"Did anything stand out? On the way, while you were there..." Jake now was at full attention in his chair, leaning forward. Hands wrapped around his coffee mug, his eyes searched Tara's face.

Tara slowly nodded. "I went the shortcut. Remember the hole?"

Jake and Ryan nodded. Tara closed her eyes, bringing

up the image her mind had given her while she was sleeping. "There was a little girl in the hole, crying for help. But she wasn't really there. It was like a memory or something I had seen before."

"But you've been never to this area?" Jake asked.

Ryan shrugged. "We went by there the first day we went to the house. Could it just be from that?"

Tara glanced at him. "I'm not sure. It could be. I remember saying that day that it all looked familiar."

"Then what?" Jake broke in.

Tara smiled. "Always in a hurry." She took a deep breath. "It was weird. I remember looking up at the house from the house and just feeling the anger coming from it. Cecilia was beside me telling me she wanted to show me something upstairs and I went with her. The stairs and foyer were lit up like it was a bright, sunny day. But when I got to the top of the stairs, it was dark. She led me to a room at the end of the hall and disappeared through it."

"Wait," Jake broke in. "You could see her?"

Tara nodded slowly. "Yes, at that moment. Not complete features, but a young girl about my age, dressed in blue. She was giggly. She laced her arm through mine and walked with me like she was showing me some secret. But when we got to the door, she went right into the room, but the door was locked."

"So you didn't see or feel anything else?" Ryan murmured.

"I could hear Cecilia laughing and I swear I could hear crying faintly from someone else. But then my grandmother showed up and told me I didn't want to go in there. She directed me back here." Tara shivered. "I came to at the edge of the woods when it started raining. I ran home from there." It dawned on Tara that she had called this place home and the irony wasn't lost on her that she really didn't have a home.

"I wish we had been with you," Ryan said.

Jake nodded. "There's definitely something odd going on here, and it isn't just Cecilia in that house."

Tara pushed the empty mug aside. "It definitely sounded like there was at least one other voice. But who is it?"

Jake shrugged. "We need to figure out who has lived there since Cecilia."

"What if she tormented other people while they lived there?" Ryan asked.

Jake started laughing.

"What's so funny?" Ryan demanded.

"A month ago that question never would have come out of your mouth."

Ryan snorted. "Trust me, I can't believe I even think that is a possibility."

"Looks like you have your work cut out for you at the historical society." Tara sat forward. "I want to go with you."

Jake nodded. "They should be open tomorrow." He glanced down at his watch. It was now five a.m. "How about breakfast?"

Ryan and Tara both nodded. "Pancakes?" Tara asked.

"You've got it. Go rest in the living room and I'll get them started."

Tara went into the living room and sat down on the couch. She pulled the blanket on the back of it down on top of her and curled up. Ryan had stayed in the kitchen to help Jake and she smiled as she listened to their banter. From the sounds of it, they were making a huge breakfast, with Ryan starting bacon and potatoes.

Tara stared into space and cleared her mind. She closed her eyes and called for her grandmother. Silence. She cried out mentally, *Gram, please come to me.*

Again, there was silence except for the distant sounds from the kitchen. She opened her eyes and swallowed hard down the tears that threatened. She had followed her grandmother's advice to come here, to seek whoever he was out, which she still hadn't been able to do, and now her grandmother was leaving her alone. Why? She had grown up talking to her grandmother on the phone, but she couldn't remember what she looked like. She didn't know if she had ever seen her or met her in person. There had been no pictures in the house of her grandmother. Tara wracked her brain, trying to remember her grandmother's eyes, hair, anything that she could recognize. Tears welled up in her eyes as fear gripped her at the realization *there was nothing.*

Chapter Twenty-Three

As bacon cooked in the oven, Ryan diced up potatoes and placed them in a skillet with some diced onion and garlic. He covered the pan and turned towards Jake. "I'm concerned about her."

Jake nodded. "I know. I am too. Is this sleepwalking new and, if so, what triggered it?"

Ryan turned back to the stove and stirred the potatoes to make sure they weren't sticking to the pan. "We have got to figure out what is going on, man. Or we'll be taking turns sitting downstairs to follow her if she continues to sleepwalk."

Jake flipped pancakes on a griddle and nodded. "The fact that now she is hearing another voice at the house concerns me. What if there are multiple ghosts there? Are they all angry like Cecilia, or is she keeping them there, tormenting them with her anger?"

Ryan let out a hiss. "This is getting out of control, and I'm afraid someone is going to get hurt. We know Cecilia would hurt me in a heartbeat just because I look like an ancestor she was married to."

"But would she hurt Tara if she feels she is protecting Tara from you?" Jake asked as he stacked up the cooked pancakes. Both men were silent as they finished cooking breakfast. After heaping three plates with food, they went to the living room to find Tara sitting on the couch, tears running down her face.

"What's wrong?" Ryan asked as he placed her place along with his on the coffee table in front of the couch.

Tara wiped her eyes. "I just am trying so hard to remember my childhood and I'm just frustrated because nothing seems to bring back any memories." She reached for her plate of food.

Ryan and Jake exchanged glances. "You can't expect everything to come flooding back. It's been years," Ryan said.

Tara nodded. "I know, but it's still frustrating."

Jake stopped eating for a second. "How long has it been since you lost your memory?"

Tara sighed. "I remember nothing before I was ten. And that year was more of a blur. I remember small things, but not the entire year. Memories are much clearer from my eleventh birthday to the present."

"Did something happen at that time?" Jake asked.

Tara took a bite of bacon and shrugged. "I was told I was caught in a house fire, and that since then I don't remember anything. But I don't even remember the fire."

They continued on eating in silence. Ryan watched Tara thoughtfully as I finished eating. "What if it was something other than the fire?"

Tara set her now empty plate on the coffee table. "What do you mean?"

"I'm not sure. Just what if something else happened

that no one wanted to tell you about? Doesn't seem like a fire would cause amnesia."

Tara stared at him. "Are you suggesting my parents lied to me about what happened?"

"I'm not saying they lied. But what if it was something they didn't want you to know...maybe to protect you? I don't know. I'm just throwing things out there."

Tara smiled. "I appreciate that, but I find it hard to believe that my parents wouldn't tell me something that so inherently changed my life."

"People do it all the time, hide the truth," Jake interjected. "And usually it is for some good reason..." He air quoted around 'good reason.'

Tara nodded slowly. "I suppose. But the question then becomes how do we find out what that could be, or if they even lied to me at all? My parents have been gone for a lot of years now and my grandmother too. I don't even remember ever seeing my grandmother. There were no pictures of her, and we talked on the phone regularly, so I know her voice, but I couldn't tell you what she looked like."

Ryan reached for her hand. "That must be disconcerting, especially if you were close to her. Do you think it was always that way or was that just since the amnesia came?"

Tara shook her head. "I honestly don't know. Maybe I knew what she looked like when I was younger, but it seems impossible now to remember that."

"What do we know about the Holden House? Other than it last belonged to some old crazy lady that people thought was a witch?" Tara changed the subject.

"Nothing really. We need to find out who used to live there and go back in history," Jake answered. "I really am curious as to if there are more spirits than just Cecilia there."

Ryan shivered. "I'm not sure I want to find that out, especially if they all hate the Stafford family like apparently she does."

Tara laughed softly. "I never took you for a chicken. Where is your sense of adventure?"

"You and I have very different ideas of what an adventure is." Ryan grabbed the dirty places from the table and reached for Jake's. He headed to the kitchen, leaving Tara and Jake in the living room.

Tara watched him leave before turning towards Jake. "When can we go to the historical society?"

Jake glanced at his watch. "Another two hours and Hester will be there. She's the one I've been told to talk to. Apparently, she knows the most history surrounding this town." He pulled the ottoman closer to him and placed his feet up. "Why do you feel there is a tie here to you and the Holden House?"

"I don't know. I can't put my finger on it. But my grandmother seems to have led me to this place. I just don't know why, or who she is...or who I am, for that matter. It never bothered me, but lately, my lack of memories seems to be more evident and really grating on my nerves." Tara watched Jake. "Why are you doing this?"

Jake smiled. "Because I had a friend in need and when he called, I came. The supernatural has always fascinated me. Ryan knew that. He was concerned for you."

"Just seems odd that you would jump so naturally into this and put your life on hold."

Jake shrugged. "My life isn't on hold. I'm a PI by occupation. This is just a pro bono case." He grinned at her.

"Call it satisfying an itch for me. I'm always looking for supernatural stuff to get involved in for fun."

Tara laid on her side and tucked a pillow under her head, struggling to keep her eyes open. "Sorry. I need to get a catnap in before we go talk with Hester." She hadn't closed her eyes more than five minutes when she fell into a dreamless sleep. Her last thoughts were of hoping Cecilia and her grandmother would let her sleep.

Chapter Twenty-Four

TARA DIDN'T SLEEP MORE THAN TWENTY MINUTES AND WHEN she awoke, she was alone in the living room. The house was quiet. She rose and went to the kitchen, but it was empty. She started upstairs and shivered at the oppressive silence. She went to Ryan's door, which was open and the room empty. Same with Jake's.

She turned toward her own room. Grabbing her laptop, she started back downstairs with the intent to head to the porch to do some research. She heard a thud coming from above her and she turned, eyes traveling to the ceiling. *The attic.* She turned and made her way to the attic door at the end of the hall. It was ajar and as she pulled it open, she heard Jake and Ryan talking.

"We don't know for sure what happened to the deed," Ryan stated.

"But we do know that at some point it transferred back to the Holden family after Cecilia died."

"Yes, but not sure how long after her death. Records are hard to find from that time. Everything is digitized now, but things before the 1900s are hard to find. If it was written, they get misplaced, fires happened..."

Tara stood at the bottom of the stairs. She felt like an intruder for some reason, but weren't they all in this together? But if the house had left the Stafford family, was there a rift in the families? Especially after Cecilia's death. She backed away from the door and turned to go downstairs. Maybe this was a conversation Ryan didn't want to share with her and she would wait until he said something. If he didn't, was there something he was hiding? After all, she didn't know him that well.

She felt the anxiety bubble up inside her as she hurried down the stairs and out onto the porch. She flopped into a chair and just concentrated on slowing her breathing. She would not allow the panic attack to overtake her. So she didn't known Ryan that well. He had been nothing but nice to her. Kind, loving even. And Jake had become a friend also. They seemed to have her best interest at hand, but what was her best interest? Was it just finding out who this mystery man was that had brought her here? Or was it finding out who she was? Did her grandmother bring her all this way to guide her to finding her memories and find out who she truly was? What had she lost all these years without knowing her true identity?

Tara sighed. She had never been this bothered by the lack of memories. When her parents died, she almost felt relieved that she couldn't remember everything. Her mom's last words to her was the truth will come out eventually. Tara hadn't known what she was talking about at the time, but now she sat here at the Stafford House, and wondered what that truth was and was it tied to this town, the Staffords and the Holdens.

She opened her computer and immediately opened the Ancestry file. She typed in Shetfield and there was nothing. Shetfield was a paternal name. It didn't seem to be recognized at all in the ancestry database. *How odd.* Tara sat staring into space. She tried variations of the spelling of it and still nothing came up. She opened a google search tab and started a search for Shetfield. Again, it revealed nothing. Tara cursed under her breath. She had never run into such a dead end like this whenever she did research.

She went back to the ancestry database. She put in her father's name, Paul Shetfield. *Nothing.* She tried her mother's name, Peggy Shetfield. *Nothing.* She put in her own name, Tara Shetfield. *Nothing.* Her chest tightened as the realization washed over her that maybe these were not their names. Who were her parents? Who was she? She wracked her brain for her grandmother's name, but couldn't remember. Gram. That was all Tara had ever called her. She closed her laptop with a snap and closed her eyes. The longing for family had never been so strong within her.

"Hey," Jake's soft whisper broke through her thoughts and Tara opened her eyes.

"Where were you?" Tara asked.

"Attic with Ryan. He's still up there going through his grandfather's stuff." Jake gestured towards the sidewalk. "Ready to go hear some history of this town?"

"I am. Let me just throw my laptop inside." Tara rose.

They walked quietly down the street toward the historical society. As they arrived, Hester was just opening up.

Jake introduced the two of them and told Hester they

had been referred to her for some historical information on the Holden House.

Tara thought she saw the lady flinch at the mention of the Holden House, but if it happened, she had recovered quickly and led them inside. They settled around a round table in the building's corner and Hester looked at both of them.

"Why are you interested in the Holden House?" she asked.

Jake looked at Tara and then back to Hester. "It's a curious place and I have a fascination with the supernatural. I was told there was a possibility of a spirit or two lurking about." He smiled as if he was half-joking.

Hester scoffed. "There is no such thing as ghosts. You would be well advised to put that nonsense out of your head."

Tara leaned forward. "That silliness aside..." She shook her head at Jake. "Can you tell us of the history of the house? I saw the outside and it must have been a real beauty in its day."

Hester frowned at Jake. "Of course. The house was part of the Holden estate in the 1800s. When Cecilia Holden married, it was part of her dowry."

"And who did she marry?" Tara asked. She glanced down at her hands and saw that her phone was recording as she had intended.

"Oh, it was the biggest wedding in this parts in that day. She married into the Stafford family. You might know the family home for the Staffords. I believe a young man named Ryan Stafford still lives there."

"Yes, I know the house. It's beautiful. Almost as beautiful as the Holden House must have been." Tara tried to steer back toward the reason they were here.

Hester nodded. "Yes. Poor Cecilia. She died quite young. She was only twenty-five."

Tara made the appropriate sympathy noises. "How did she die? Must have been childbirth in that time."

Hester sighed. "That would have been better than what really happened. Unfortunately, she killed herself."

Tara's eyes widened. "How?"

Hester frowned. "That is unknown. There was a lot of speculation, but we never could find any proof of anything."

"So you are just assuming she died from a broken heart?" Jake asked.

"Unsure really, but her husband had a child born with his second wife about six months after her death so it can be speculated that he was stepping out on her."

"Not unheard of in that time that a man would take a mistress," Jake said.

"No, it's not. But it's not common for the husband to marry said mistress if she was pregnant," Hester replied.

"So did the Holden House stay in the Stafford family after her death? It surely wouldn't continue to be called Holden House if that was the case," Tara asked.

Hester shook her head. "It stayed with the Stafford family until Brandon died in 1875. He had four children by then and his wife, Hattie, was unable to care for the house financially. She claimed unusual disturbances in the house, but really she was half mad and drunk most of the time. Her children, so it is said, suffered terribly. She sold the house back to the Holdens in order to move and make a new life for her and her kids. Only one of the children returned when they were in their late teens and stayed local after that."

Tara nodded. "So the house went back to the Holden family. Who lived in it after it was taken back?"

Hester stood and went to a shelf, where she pulled out an enormous book. "This is the Holden family history. It looks like Orrin, Cecilia's brother, took it over when he got married in 1878. It continued to be passed down to his son, William, to William's son Albert, to Albert's son Grant and there it went to back to Grant's mother, Priscilla. Now it is technically owned by Priscilla's granddaughter, Anna, but last I knew they still had yet to locate her. If they don't locate her by her twenty-fifth birthday, then it will be sold at auction."

Tara nodded. "Wow, this is incredible. What do you know about this Anna?"

Hester shook her head. "Nothing. I never knew her. I remember Priscilla as she was the last person to live there, but she was a recluse mostly and few people in the town actually interacted with her."

Jake had been silent for the most part, and now Tara looked at him. He was watching her. "I met Anna a couple of times. We were just kids, but her folks lived here in town. You must have records of her parents."

Hester consulted the book and after flipping a few pages, found what she was looking for. "Here it is. Her parents were David and Paula Holden. Anna was an only child. David was Albert's son. The last record I have of them was that they are deceased, but not notation of how they died. Apparently they moved away years before they passed on."

Tara sat forward. "And no record of Anna?"

"No. She apparently dropped off the face of the earth. Well, I can say we have a few years were records weren't being updated so that is probably why we lost track of her." She smiled sadly. "There is only so much a historian can do."

Jake and Tara stood and thanked Hester for her time.

Chapter Twenty-Five

TARA WAS BURSTING BY THE TIME THEY LEFT THE BUILDING. She could hardly contain herself. As they started down the sidewalk, she reached for Jake's arm. "We have to go to the house."

Jake laughed. "You are like a kid at Christmas. Right now? You don't want to talk to Ryan first and fill him in on what you found out."

"What *we* found out. And yes, and no. I really want to go talk to Cecilia. Maybe I can text him and have him meet us there." She smiled up at him before pulling out her phone.

Jake put his hand over the phone and stopped her. "I think it's important we regroup with Ryan and see what everyone has for information. Ryan might have found something also."

Tara looked up quizzically. "You sure?"

Jake nodded and started walking back towards the Stafford House. Tara let out a sigh, but turned to fall into step with him. Her mind was reeling. She wanted to let Cecilia know she understood the pain she must have been feeling to end her life the way she did. What a scoundrel this Brandon had been and, oh my God, the hurt that Cecilia must have felt. No wonder she was so angry at Ryan.

"What if Cecilia doesn't want Ryan at the house? It might be safer for him for us to go," Tara said.

"Maybe, but don't you think that should be Ryan's decision?"

Tara huffed. Yes, it should be his decision, but she was bursting at the seams to get to the house. This seemingly unnecessary detour was killing her. Stafford House came into view and Tara paused. She had seen this house a hundred times, walked in and out of it, and yet for the first time she realized how majestic this house appeared compared to the ones around her. It was old, as old as Holden House, and yet having been maintained over the years left it looking every bit incredible for its age.

"You okay?" Jake turned toward her.

She nodded. "I was just really looking at the house. It's amazing how well it has endured the years and still can inspire awe from those who pass by it."

Jake looked at the house. "Can you imagine if Holden House had been maintained like this one?"

A *yes* escaped from her and she linked her arm through Jake's. "Let's go get the caretaker of this incredible beauty."

Jake's laughter filled the street as they walked arm and arm up the porch steps. "You realize no one talks like that...weirdo."

Tara stuck out her tongue at him and burst into the house. "Ryan?"

Ryan came out of the living room. "What did you find?"

Jake and Tara settled into the living room and related the news that Hester had shared with them. Ryan looked between the two. It was a lot of information.

"Where do we go from here?" He finally asked.

"I think we should go talk to Cecilia. I wasn't sure you would want to go with because of the way she feels about Brandon...and rightly so, and how much you look like him. But Jake thought you should decide that." Tara grinned at Ryan.

"Oh, you were going to make that decision for me?" Ryan wasn't sure whether to be grateful or ticked off about that.

"I was thinking of your safety. We know now why Cecilia is so angry. I would want to kill you too if I thought you were Brandon," Tara pointed out.

"True," Ryan conceded. "But I want to go."

Jake broke in. "Did you find anything?"

Ryan shook his head. "Not really. I found a copy of the deed, but it didn't show that it was signed back over to the Holdens. But it was just a copy and it could have been from the original transfer when Brandon and Cecilia got married."

"What is it you think you will find in your grandfather's papers? Do they go back even into the 1800s?" Tara asked.

"No. And I don't know." Ryan ran a hand through his hair. "The papers upstairs are from his time as a lawyer, but there is a folder regarding the Holdens." He pointed to the coffee table. A fair thick folder sat on the table. Tara hadn't noticed it before, but she had been excited about the news from the historical society.

Tara glanced from the folder to Ryan. He gestured for her to go ahead and pick it up. She reached for it and sat back. As she opened it slowly, there were newspaper articles cut out, handwritten ledger sheets, wedding announcements, birth announcements, all of the members that Hester had just told them about. "Why did he keep all this?"

Ryan shook his head. "I have no idea."

Tara scooted over on the couch closer to Ryan as Jake made his way over to sit next to her. They looked over the documents, occasionally pointing out a name that they had just heard about. The genealogy chart was fully filled out, right down to Anna. There was another one for the Stafford family that showed Brandon at the top and continued through the years down until Ryan and his brother, Geoffrey. "This is amazing," Tara gushed.

"The question is what does all this mean?" Ryan asked.

Jake looked up. "Does it have to mean anything? Maybe the families were just intertwined enough that your grandfather was interested...from a town historical point of view. Staffords and Holdens were the two big families of the town."

"Maybe." Ryan stood and started pacing around the living room.

Tara watched him off and on as she continued to go through the file. Near the back of the file was a wedding announcement of Albert Holden and Priscilla, Anna's grandmother. "Look, this is Anna's grandparents." She continued to turn pages. "I would have hoped there had been one of Anna's parents."

Ryan sighed. "I noticed that there was nothing after her grandparents. Only the birth announcements of their two sons, Grant and David."

Tara sat back and Jake slid the folder off her lap onto

his. He finished his pursual of the papers. The last paper he picked up was a small one that had been attached to another paper. He pulled out a small section of newspaper that was an obituary. "This is Priscilla's obituary. So sad that it was only a paragraph long."

"It's like the whole family just faded away. No information on her sons, no information on Anna's parents." Tara sighed. "Why didn't your grandfather have that information if he has her obit?"

Ryan shrugged. "I don't know. I have no idea as to why he kept this information. There has to be some reason."

Tara stood up. "I think the answers are at the Holden House. We need to go back there."

They all agreed that they would go there this afternoon. Jake wanted to call and ask questions of a friend who had dealings with the supernatural. Tara and Ryan gathered together a bag of flashlights that would give them enough hours if they stayed there for a while. Tara was determined to stay until they had some answers.

"The place needs to be searched from top to bottom," she declared. Ryan rolled his eyes.

They had a light lunch and each of them returned to their rooms to change into comfy clothes and grab a sweatshirt in case of a sudden change of temperature in the house. Tara knew Ryan was nervous, but gave him kudos for wanting to go along on this outing. She would be terrified if she was in his shoes.

She closed her eyes as she sat on her bed. *Gram, if you can hear me, be with us tonight. Allow us to talk to Cecilia.*

She opened her eyes and found Ryan standing at the door of her room. He was waiting quietly. She nodded and stood up. They found Jake by the front door, bag of flashlights in hand. They walked out the door and into the late afternoon sun. It was now four p.m. and Tara was practically skipping down the sidewalk with her excitement.

They arrived in record time to the Holden House and Tara stopped short with the guys coming up quickly behind her. She looked up at the house. The disrepair couldn't hide the fact that this house had been glorious in its day. The other night when she looked at it in her sleepwalking haze, it had been angry, but now all she saw was sadness. She stared up at the windows on the second floor overlooking the veranda. They were dark and gloomy. Not a sign of life behind them, or a spirit for that matter.

They moved around to the back of the house to the back door that they had been using. Tara once again looked up, but this time she could swear she saw a curtain move. *Cecilia, I need to talk to you.* She prayed her silent call was heard. She was the first one in the house and stood for a moment in the kitchen. Nothing had changed here. They hadn't really touched anything and she went over to the cupboards and opened doors. All was empty except a few dishes and glassware.

She stared at the basement door at the end of the kitchen. "Let's start there," she pointed to the door.

Both Ryan and Jake looked at each other and nodded. Jake handed her a flashlight. "Let me go first."

Tara nodded. Ryan gestured for her to follow Jake, allowing himself to fall into step behind her. They each had a flashlight and proceeded down the stairs in a single line. Ryan was careful to leave the door open and had even stuck a small rock in the casing so the door wouldn't shut tight if it for some reason slammed behind them.

Arriving at the bottom of the stairs, they fanned out and swung their flashlights into different corners. The floor was dirt and over the years, areas of ground water found its way to the surface. They walked around the dry areas. Nothing was in the basement. The walls were covered with moss where it had become overgrown.

They started back up the stairs and stopped halfway up when they all heard a creaking board above them. It came from the hallway, from the kitchen to the front of the house. Jake was first headed up the stairs and he proceeded quietly, one step at a time. Another floorboard creaked as if someone was stepping on it. Jake came into the kitchen and swung his light down the hallway. Nothing, no one. The hall was empty.

"Cecilia?" Tara called out.

A girlish giggle floated down the hall to them and Tara started forward. Jake and Ryan tried to stop her, but in the end just followed her. Tara followed the giggle until she got to the stairway. She glanced up the stairs and once again it was dark. She shined the light up, and a glimpse of movement caught her eye. She started up the stairs before Jake or Ryan could say a word.

"Cecilia, wait," she called out.

Catch me, the voice came back to Tara. Tara sighed.

"I don't want to play games, Cecilia. I need to talk to you. I know what happened."

Come with me, the voice was down the hallway now and Tara swung her light back and forth trying to see the full hallway. Suddenly it was illuminated with Ryan and Jake standing next to her, both of them holding a flashlight in each hand. Between the five lights, the hallway lit up. There was no movement, but Tara could hear the giggle.

"Do you guys hear that?" she whispered.

Jake nodded and Ryan shook his head and said, "Damn, just let me know if she is coming at me."

Jake snorted. "We hear her, can't see her, dude."

Jake groaned. "Of course."

Tara moved forward into the hallway. She focused her light in on the door that had been locked when she was sleepwalking. She got to it and laid her ear against it. Once again, she could hear soft crying. She jumped when she heard a voice next to her other ear. *I never hurt her, just scared her.*

"Cecilia." Tara turned and demanded, "Let me see you."

Ryan and Jake were about five feet from her when suddenly her light caught a flash of blue. Tara trained her light in on where she had seen the flash. A shimmering translucent blue waxed and waned within the light. Tara stepped closer. The blue darkened just a bit while the face of a young girl with blond hair came into focus.

"Who didn't you hurt?" Tara asked.

He brought her into this house. My house. Tara shuddered, knowing instinctively that she was talking about Brandon's mistress.

"What did you do?" Tara asked, taking another step forward.

I did nothing, just scared her. She wasn't the one I wanted to hurt.

"Did you hurt Brandon?" Tara tried to remember what Hester had said about Brandon and when he had died. She couldn't recall the details around his death, only that he had left four children.

Brandon took a fall down the stairs. Cecilia moved

toward the stairs, brushing against Ryan. Ryan paled and Tara took another step forward.

"Are you okay?" she asked Ryan.

He nodded. "Just a chill."

Tara turned her attention back to Cecilia. "What do you mean he took a fall?"

Same fall HE will take. A translucent finger pointed to Ryan.

"Why? He has done nothing to you?"

Hasn't he? He is just like Brandon. Charming, good-looking...looks just like him actually. He will break your heart.

"My decision. Not yours." Tara clenched her teeth, holding back the *you bitch* she wanted to scream. The thought of something happening to Ryan chilled Tara to the bone and she pushed through the fearful thoughts.

Your love for him cannot sustain a relationship. Trust me on this, Cecilia went on.

Jake had turned toward Ryan and was explaining quietly what Cecilia was saying. Tara shook her head. "You don't know how he feels."

Do you? He will ply you with pretty lies that will cloud your judgment. In the end, you will be the one left dead, or near dead at the heartbreak he has caused.

Tara shook her head. "What about her?" Tara pointed to the room at the end of the hall.

What about her? She left willingly, although a bit mad or so the towns people thought. She never did recover from her husband's death, I'm afraid. The laughter that came from her was icy and even Tara shivered at the chill that filled the air. The house was freezing now and Tara moved closer to Ryan and Jake. They closed in together in a tight circle, trying to draw warmth from each other.

Chapter Twenty-Six

THE SIGHT OF CECILIA HAD DISAPPEARED AND THE HALLWAY slowly started losing the chill. Ryan turned toward Tara. "Is she gone?"

"For the moment." Tara was irritated and strode to the door at the end of the hall. She twisted the handle and the door flew open. Odd. It had been locked the other night. Tara stepped into the room and looked around. It was empty. Not one piece of furniture sat in the room. She turned around slowly in the middle of the room, taking in every inch of the place. The walls had a pale yellow wallpaper that was tearing off the walls in chunks. Was this the work of Cecilia, or of the new wife losing her mind because of Cecilia's torment? On the far wall, the wallpaper hung in a strip, slowing making its way to the floor. Tara walked over and tore it off the wall, flinging it behind her.

Ryan and Jake stood just inside the door. She glanced at them and turned toward the window. She wiped the grim away in a spot and looked out. It looked over the far side of the building where it was mostly woods. Tara stared out the window. A small light shone through the trees, bobbing along as if being held and moving with each step. She motioned for the boys to come closer.

"Do you see that?" She asked.

Both peered out the window. Ryan shook his head. Like usual, he wasn't privy to these things. Jake nodded. "If Ryan can't see it, you know it's a spirit. No offense, man."

Ryan gave a hollow laugh. "I'm not sure if that is a curse or a blessing at this point."

She used to walk out there. Thought it would protect her from what was in here, the voice whispered next to Tara and Tara jumped.

"Can you not leave the house?" she asked.

No. I'm bound here. But anyone who enters is fair game for my wrath.

Tara closed her eyes. *Gram, where are you?*

She's not available to talk to you right now, Cecilia broke into Tara's thoughts.

"What did you do with her?"

Cecilia's laughter filled the room and even Ryan jumped. He glanced around. "I heard that."

I didn't do anything to her. We coexisted very peacefully for years. She allowed me to roam freely as long as I left her alone. She sympathized with me really, but she was bound to protect you.

"Wait. My grandmother never lived here."

Oh, my dear. Of course she did. She wanted you to be with him. The wallpaper Tara had thrown on the floor, whisked through the air and wrapped around Ryan.

"She didn't know Ryan. What are you talking about?"

You do not understand. You need to learn more about your life. Go to the study. Remember the corridor.

Tara turned to Ryan as he was pulling the wallpaper off him and dropping it on the floor. "I take it this was her throwing it at me?" Ryan asked, irritation lacing his words.

Tara nodded. "We need to go down to the study. Where I found the secret passage...the answers are there, according to Cecilia."

Tara strode from the room without looking back. Jake and Ryan followed at her heels. Tara walked into the study and looked around. Nothing had changed in the few days she had been in here. "She mentioned the secret passage." Tara stepped to the bookcase and found the concealed switch that pushed the bookcase into the wall. She turned. "I think we need to search every aspect of this room.

Jake moved toward the desk. He pulled open the first drawer and there saw a photo of young Anna. He pulled it out and handed it to Ryan. Tara peered at the photo. A flicker of a memory that she couldn't quite place crossed her mind. Jake continued to rummage through the drawers, but found nothing other than a few receipts and odd papers. Nothing that meant anything to either Tara or Ryan. Ryan had moved to the other side of the room and was looking at the books in the bookcase. The shelves held only a few books, yet he was running his fingers along the wood.

"There has to be other passages like that one," he said. "They probably connect different parts of the house."

Tara stepped over next to him and ran her fingers along the side panels where the first trigger had been. There was nothing. "Maybe there is only one entrance per room."

"Well, let's see where this one goes. Maybe that will give us a better indication of what we should be looking for," Ryan said.

The three turned back to the passage and stepped through. It was dusty and cobwebs hung from the corners. The illumination from their three flashlights was bright and gave the trio a sense of confidence that each individually wouldn't have had in the dark. Jake took the lead with Tara and Ryan holding hands following. Tara noticed the excitement in Jake's steps and how he swung his light into every shadow. She smiled to herself as she realized just how much he lived for this sort of stuff.

The passage wasn't wide like a normal hallway. Tara and Ryan had no problem walking side by side, but it was tight and as they got a curve, they would have to stagger a bit to walk comfortably. They got to an intersection in the corridor. Jake shone his light down one side and Tara and Ryan shone theirs down the other. Neither side could see the end of it.

"Do we separate and see where they go?" Jake asked. "We can cover more ground."

Tara looked back and forth between Jake and Ryan. "Do you think that's smart?"

"I think Cecilia sent you here so there is something we should be looking for." Jake pulled out his phone and opened the walkie-talkie feature. Ryan did the same. "We can communicate with each other with these."

Tara nodded. "Okay. You take that one and we'll go this way. If you find another room, let us know."

They parted ways. Tara and Ryan moved down the hallway until it came to what appeared to be a dead end. "This can't be right," Tara commented.

They searched every angle of the wall, looking for

some sort of catch that would reveal a door. This space was a bit narrower than previously and they stood single file.

Ryan clicked the walkie. "We hit a dead end."

The phone crackled as Jake came through. "Come this way. I think I might have found something."

The two hustled back through the corridor until they caught up with Jake. Jake was standing in a small space that had widened out so the three could fit comfortably together. To the right of the room was a wooden door that didn't have a handle. Tara ran her fingers over it, finding no latch that would open it.

"Another dead end?"

Jake shook his head. "It goes somewhere. We just have to figure out how to open it." He turned his flashlight to the other side of the enclosure. There stood three wooden crates that were covered with dust and grim in a stack, obviously untouched for many years. The trio moved over to them and looked them over. The tops were nailed on and would require a crowbar to pry them open. Ryan pushed on the top one. As it moved an inch, a *whoosh* sounded behind them. They turned to find the door had opened.

"Well, well. I guess the crates are the trigger." Tara smiled and started toward the door. She stepped through into a small sitting room. She didn't remember seeing this room when they had explored the house. There were two small wing-backed chairs whose color had faded beyond recognition. The seating and back's velvet had long since started to deteriorate and stuffing jutted from different holes in the fabric.

Tara stepped closer and ran a finger along one of them. She turned toward the fireplace where the chairs had been placed close by. It had been used in years past and she wondered just when was the last time someone had sat here next to a lit fire, warming themselves, perhaps reading a book or having an intimate conversation with the one they loved. She turned to see Ryan on the far wall, where a table stood. He was staring at something on the table and Tara walked over to see what he was looking at. Jake had gone to another corner and was looking through a steamer trunk.

Before Tara reached Ryan, Jake called to both of them to come over. "Check this out."

They accommodated him and saw in the trunk gowns that had seen better days, and yet were well-preserved considering how many years they had been sitting there. "Do you think these were Cecilia's?" Tara asked.

Jake nodded. "I would imagine so. Why else would she send us here?"

"Maybe because of the envelope on the table," Ryan said.

Tara looked at the table. "What was it?"

Ryan walked back over and picked it up. He handed it to Tara. "It's addressed to Anna."

"Should I open it?" Tara looked at Ryan. "She was your friend."

"I think you should open it. It may have answers you are looking for."

Tara looked down at the envelope and slid a finger under the flap. The adhesive had long since dried out and it flipped open with no effort. Before Tara could pull the contents out, all the flashlights flickered and went out. Tara could hear Jake hitting it against his hand. Tara pulled out her phone and hit the button for the flashlight. It didn't turn on.

A cool breeze swirled around Tara, and she reached out into the dark. Suddenly, the breeze was gone, and the flashlights illuminated once again. Tara glanced over at Jake and then at Ryan who were fine, but when she turned toward the door, it was closed.

"Damn it, Cecilia," Tara said under her breath, and she made her way to the door. She pulled at the edges, but there was no handle and there was no way to get a grip on it. "We need to find a way to open this door."

They started searching the room. There didn't appear to be another door out, which meant this room was part of the secret passage. Tara set the envelope on the table and turned to survey the room. Ryan and Jake had already started running their hands along the walls. Tara moved toward the fireplace. She ran her hand along the mantle and found nothing.

"Why would she shut us in here?" Tara asked. "She obviously sent us here."

"Maybe that is why she sent us here, just to lock us away so we die a slow, horrible death of starvation," Ryan replied.

Jake chuckled. "She would do that to you, but I doubt she would leave Tara here like that."

Tara sighed. Closing her eyes, she willed her grandmother to come to her. Several moments passed while Tara stood there with her eyes closed. She heard the guys stop moving and assumed they were just watching her. *Gram? Please.*

A warm sensation wrapped around Tara. It settled around her like a blanket and just stayed a few minutes. As it lifted, Tara heard her. *Forget the door. The only latch to open it is on the other side. Come with me.* She felt the warm sensation pull her toward the trunk in the corner. *Push it aside.*

Tara pushed at the trunk and as it moved, a small deviation in the wall became obvious. Jake came to her side and started examining it. "What did your grandmother tell you to do?"

Push on it. Tara pushed on the wall, and it gave way to another room. The opening was small and they would have to crouch to go through. Tara started forward and stopped. "Grab the envelop, Ryan."

The trio moved forward into the next room and found themselves in the cramped space under the stairs. Jake was able to open the door that went into the hallway and they all tumbled out, dusty and disheveled. They brushed themselves off and looked around. "What was the purpose of that?" Ryan demanded.

Tara shrugged. "I'm not sure Cecilia has a purpose other than tormenting people." A rush of cool air chilled Tara as she spoke. "Let's get out of here. I've had enough for tonight."

There was no argument from Jake or Ryan and they left the house, deciding to take the long way home. They walked in silence for the most part, and Tara struggled to find the meaning of everything that had happened tonight. The air was cool, but in an inviting way, and Tara looked up to see a sky filled with stars. The prior night's rain had gone and left clear skies. Tara wished her mind was as clear as the sky. Neither of the men spoke, and she could only assume they were trying to sort the events of the night as well. She was dying to know what was in the envelope they had found in the secret room. Why would Cecilia lead them to it, especially when it was addressed to Anna? Anna owned this house. Was Tara here just because Cecilia needed closure from Brandon? How were Ryan and Tara connected?

She rubbed her right temple as a headache formed. "I don't know about you two, but I'm beat. I'd rather just go to bed tonight than think any more about this insanity."

"Are you okay?" Jake asked.

Tara nodded. "Slight headache from trying to make sense of it all."

"I know you get the brunt of it. I can't always hear what you hear," Jake said. "I'm assuming your grandmother was there at the end."

Tara nodded. "I don't know how, but I think Cecilia keeps her from talking to me mostly when we are in the house. Cecilia mentioned they lived together peacefully for years. I don't know why she thinks my grandmother lived there." Tara rubbed her temple again. The throbbing was going full-force now and she could feel it building to a migraine.

"We can figure this out tomorrow or even the next day. I think we all need a break, but you especially, Tara." Concern laced Ryan's words, and he placed his arm around her shoulder.

She was grateful for the support and although it was a five-minute walk, it felt like forever. With every step, the pain intensified in Tara's head and she longed to just be in bed. When they finally arrived, an exchange of unspoken words between Ryan and Jake took place. Ryan picked her up and headed up the stairs. Tara glanced over Ryan's shoulder to see Jake head to the living room, envelope in hand. Tiredness overtook her and thoughts left her mind as she laid her head against his shoulder and sighed.

Chapter Twenty-Seven

Tara had gone to bed to rest when they arrived home, leaving Jake and Ryan downstairs. She had barely laid down when sleep overtook her. Darkness surrounded, and she turned her head from side to side, searching for a light...any light. Tara felt the panic rise in her. Sleep wound itself tight around her, and Tara gasped for air as she sank deeper into the abyss.

Tara walked through a dark corridor, not knowing where it was leading, but being pulled through the maze as if attached to a cord. She reached her arms out, trying to feel the walls, but only air sifted through her fingers. Her voice was silent, although she was screaming in her mind for help. She cried out for her grandmother and begged her to come for her. A laughter filled the space around her and Tara cringed, shrinking inwardly. The malice-filled laughter had an undertone of sadness about it.

Cecilia. "What do you want from me?" Tara screamed.

All in good time...it will all be clear.

Tara winced at the words. She didn't want to wait any longer. She wanted to know who she was, where she belonged, and most of all, she wanted her life back. Not the life where she was always wondering who she was. She wanted her full time back, the memories whether good or bad. She wanted to remember her grandmother, what she looked like, who she was, and the memories she had with her. She wanted to go back to her childhood, to that day where she lost everything and remember all of it before that had disappeared. She felt the tears roll down her cheeks and brushed them aside.

She sank back to the oblivion as the thoughts left her sleepful mind.

Tara awoke an hour later. She had no memory of the dream, but was on edge. Her nerves were frayed and her head continued to pound. The weight of the day's activities clung to her. She sat up in bed and looked around the room. It was just as she left it. She heard voices coming from downstairs — Jake and Ryan. She shook her head to clear the cobwebs and stood up. She slowly descended the stairs, trying to catch what was being said below her. They were whispering, however, keeping whatever it was from her.

She swept into the living room. Both were sitting on the floor on either side of the coffee table. In front of them were stacks of ledgers. "What's this?" she asked.

Ryan glanced up. "You're awake."

She nodded and waited for more. When no further forthcoming information, she moved to the coffee table and picked up the top ledger. "What's this?" she asked again.

"They are ledgers of my grandfather's finances."

Tara opened it and flipped through the pages. She did

not know what she was looking for and slammed it shut, placing it back on the table.

"What are they for? Are they important to the Holden House?"

Ryan shrugged. "I honestly don't know. I had found a letter upstairs from Mrs. Holden to my grandfather, thanking him for his help with her son and family. It was about the time Anna moved away. I thought there might be more information in one of these, but I have found nothing yet."

"Why does Anna keep coming up? We know something is going on with the Holdens and the Staffords, but to what extent and does it go all the way through the generations?"

Jake interjected. "I think it has to do with the house itself and Cecilia."

"What is it we are missing, though?" Ryan closed his eyes. Tara sat down next to him and slid her arm around him.

"Why don't we just set this aside for the night? I don't know about you, but I think a good movie might be just want we need tonight."

Jake and Ryan nodded. "Just not a ghost or paranormal thing, okay?" Ryan blurted out.

Chapter Twenty-Eight

THE EVENING BEFORE HAD BEEN A RELAXING NIGHT AS THEY had watched a movie. Now Ryan was at the Holden House, and had made his way upstairs. Cecilia seemed to have been waiting for him. Ryan pushed against the cold air that threatened to knock him down the stairs. "I am not leaving." The cold air felt like it went right through him and he gasped for air. The pain in his head started again, and he held onto the railing to stop from dropping to his knees. He wasn't giving in to this lunatic.

"Ryan?" He could hear Tara's voice downstairs and he tried to answer, but no sound came out. Instead, he heard the voice that without a doubt he knew was Cecilia.

You will not have her. You will not break her.

"I'm not trying to break her," Ryan screamed, though the words came out no more than a whisper.

I believed at one time that he felt the same way, but he broke me. Tore me to pieces from the inside out.

Ryan shook his head, trying to clear the pain and fogginess that threatened to overtake him. The icy blast pushed at him again, and he lunched for the railing, hanging on for dear life. "Stop it."

You'll be the broken one when I am done with you.

Ryan gritted his teeth and pulled with all his might to clear the stairway. He moved away from the top stair, still hanging on to the railing.

You will not get away that easily. You will find yourself at the bottom of those stairs soon.

"What good does it do for you to hurt me?" Ryan asked.

I will save her.

"Save Tara? Or is this about trying to save yourself?" Ryan jeered.

Coldness seeped through his fingers as the railing turned to ice. He let go instinctively and blew on his fingers. As soon as his hands were clear of the railing, she shoved him hard backwards and he fell to the floor. He tried to stand up, but the icy hands on his shoulders pushed him back down. "You won't get away with this."

Who's going to stop me?

Ryan shuddered. "Why do you want to hurt Tara like this?"

I'm not hurting her. She may be sad for a little bit, but in the long run she will realize she didn't love you.

"What if I love her?" Ryan asked.

You don't. You Staffords don't know how to love.

"Not all Staffords are like that. My grandparents were very much in love, and my parents. I honestly don't remember beyond my grandparents."

No. It was all a lie. No Stafford has any love.

Ryan, determined to prove her wrong, stood and grabbed ahold of the railing again. "I will prove it to you. Give me that chance."

NO.

Ryan held onto the railing with both hands as he made his way down the stairs. The cold icy fingers on his back pushed and pushed, but he held on and made it down the stairs. In a second, the coldness was gone, and he breathed out a sigh of relief.

"Where were you?" Tara came around the corner.

"I was upstairs having a friendly chat with our beloved ghost," Ryan snarked.

"Are you okay?"

Ryan nodded. He rubbed his arms to warm up.

Tara turned to him. "Wait...you said having a chat?"

"Yeah. I actually heard her this time. It was creepy. Her voice was not what I was expecting, and I don't want to use the words 'pure evil', but there was something about her that was creepy, yet sad. She's heartbroken for sure." Ryan shook his head. He blinked to erase the moisture forming in his eyes. He refused to cry over a woman that was trying to break him.

"I wish she had had a better life. What a dick this Brandon Stafford was," Tara said with disgust.

They made their way to the kitchen where Jake met them, coming up from the basement stairs. They strode out of the house, arm in arm and walked toward the woods. At the clearing, Tara turned back to face the house. The drape in an upstairs window pulled back and Tara swore she could see Cecilia in blue watching them. She placed her hand on her heart, making a solemn promise to find a way for Cecilia to be happy.

Chapter Twenty-Nine

Tara made her way upstairs. A knock on her open door pulled her from her thoughts. "Hey, you okay?" Ryan asked.

"I am. Just frustrated, I guess. I feel like it's one step forward and two steps back."

Ryan leaned against the doorframe. "Maybe we need a break from all this."

Tara watched him. "Why are you so eager for me to walk away from this?"

Ryan shook his head. "I didn't say I was eager for you to walk away, but you are exhausted and, honestly, I'm worried about you. Cecilia seems hell bent on making your life miserable...and mine."

Tara stood and walked over to him. "Which means there is something we are getting close to if she is fighting us. I need to know what it is. I think there are answers, maybe about my past. There has to be a reason my grandmother brought me here."

Ryan ran a hand up her hip to her waist. His hand was gentle and it was all Tara could do not to sigh and melt against him. Was he aware that he was doing this and distracting her from the conversation?

"Do you know what answers?" Tara asked. Her hand resting on his, stopping any motion he was making.

"Of course I do, but I don't want to see you get hurt."

"I don't think she will hurt me."

"Then I don't want to see myself get hurt and you can't say you don't think she will hurt me; she has made it quite clear that she will hurt me."

Tara nodded. "Yes, she has, but what is the reason for that? It has to be more than you look like her husband." Tara smiled. "Which really is uncanny."

Ryan grinned. "He was a great looking guy, wasn't he?" He softly kissed her as he pulled her closer. He pulled back and met her eyes. "Tell me you want this too."

She closed her eyes and willed her arms to stay at her side. Tara bit her bottom lip and opened her eyes. Ryan's blue eyes searched hers. She raised her hands to rest on his waist and pulled him closer. "Yes, I want this." She pulled his shirt free from his jeans and lifted it over his head. Throwing it to the side, she ran her hands over his rock hard abs.

Ryan grabbed her hands and lifted them above her head, pinning her to the door. His face was so close to hers, but not touching. His tongue ran over her bottom lip, and she longed for him to kiss her. Tara leaned her head forward to capture his lips, but he pulled back. "Don't rush. I think you need to learn patience."

She leaned her head against the door and closed her eyes. Torture, this was his idea of learning patience. He whispered in her ear, "Keep those eyes closed."

She sighed and forced her eyes to stay shut. Ryan kissed down her jaw, down her neck. She tilted her head to give him better access to that sweet spot between her shoulder and neck. He chuckled as he moved past the spot he knew she wanted him to be. Letting go of her hands, he ran his hands down her cheeks, her neck with his fingers dancing over her skin. Tara pushed against the door, arms still raised overhead.

Ryan ran his fingers over her taunt nipples pushing against her tank top. She moaned softly. Lifting the hem of her tank top, Ryan pulled it slowly up and stopped just above her breasts. He glanced up at her, her eyes still closed, lips parted. Kissing her softly on the lips, suckling the bottom lip into his mouth, he gently teased her nipples rolling them between his fingers. Tara whimpered softly and arched her back, wanting more.

Ryan broke off the kiss and moved to the base of her neck, licking her lightly. He yanked the tank top over her head and tossed it out of the way. He held the weight of her breasts in his hands, thumbs moving in circles over her nipples. She inhaled sharply as he took one nipple into his mouth and suckled her. Her hands made their way to his head, fingers entwining in his hair, pulling him closer.

Ryan pulled back and picked her up. Tara wrapped her arms around his neck and kissed him as he stumbled across the room to the bed where he placed her and slid her bottoms off. Tara reached for his jeans, making quick work of the button and zipper. Pulling them down off his hips, she reached for him. He closed his eyes as her hand wrapped around the length of him. He trembled and pulled back from her. Stepping out of his jeans, he pulled a condom from his back pocket.

Ryan pushed her back onto the bed. His hand slid up her thigh, finding her wet warmth. He stroked her, her eyes clouding as she went over the edge. He gently kissed her, trying to slow his breathing. "I can't wait, Tara." He sat up and rolled the protection on. Nestled between her legs, his mouth brushed hers as he slid into her heat. They moved together as one, a perfect melody played together. She clung to him as she hit her peak again and called out his name. Ryan shuddered and kissed her deeply as he rode the crest with her.

Chapter Thirty

When Tara dozed off, Ryan had tiptoed from the bed and dressed quietly. He shut the door quietly as he left the room. He then headed upstairs to the attic and his grandfather's stuff. There had to be more there. It was a feeling he had had for the past few days, but he didn't know how to bring it up to Jake or Tara, at least not until he was sure.

Rummaging through papers and files, Ryan finally found what he was looking for. He ran downstairs to find Jake and Tara in the living room. He waved papers around, excitement oozing off him.

"I found something about Anna and her family. My grandfather gave Anna's parents money for them to move., he burst out.

Tara and Jake stared at him. "Why would he do that?" Tara asked.

Ryan frowned. "There was just a duplicate check receipt and at the bottom it said 'move'."

"Okay. But why would he do that?" Jake asked.

Ryan sighed. "I don't know. I thought it might be something, but maybe not."

Jake reached for the papers. "It is something, we just don't know where it fits into the puzzle yet." Jake scanned the papers and on the last sheet, he put it on the coffee table. "Did you read these pages?"

"No, I found the duplicate check, and I just grabbed everything behind it in the folder." Ryan grinned.

Jake rolled his eye. "Look at this last page. It looks like it may have come from a journal or something."

Ryan and Tara leaned over the table to read it.

I don't know how to save the girl. All I know is it is impossible for them to stay here. My family started this and it's time for me to try and right the wrong. I gave David money today and told them to get far away from here. Ryan's devastated, but it is for the best if Anna is to survive this blasted curse. I put them in touch with a doctor who can use hypnotism to help her forget everything. She will remember only what they tell her going forward. It's a terrible thing. She will never remember Ryan. I almost wish I could do the same for Ryan so he doesn't suffer.

Tara sat back and watched Ryan. He fought back the urge to bolt from the room. His grandfather paid his best friend's parents to move and to basically make sure she forgot her childhood. He looked at Tara. She had a tear running down her cheek.

"What are you thinking?" he asked her.

"That poor girl. She would have had similar experiences to me not remembering."

Jake cleared his throat. "I hate to be the voice of reason here, but have either of you thought Tara could actually be Anna? I'm assuming if her parents erased her memories, then they would have given her a new identity."

"But I don't recognize any of the pictures of Anna. Wouldn't I recognize myself?"

Jake shook his head. "Maybe not. Not if you saw no pictures of yourself as a child. You said it yourself; you don't remember ever seeing your grandmother, just talked to her on the phone so you know her voice."

Ryan sat down next to Tara on the couch. "You remember nothing?"

Tara shook her head. "Can you undergo hypnosis to bring back memories?"

"Possibly." Jake sat forward. "I have a friend that has undergone hypnosis for smoking cessation; I can see if I can get a hold of his hypnotist's information and we can always call and ask."

Tara nodded. "I think we should try it. What do we have to lose?"

Ryan reached for her hand. "I'm sorry, Tara. If this is my grandfather's doing, I'm so sorry."

"We don't know it is. We don't know that Anna is me, or I'm Anna." Tara shrugged. "The important thing is I think this is a big part of the puzzle and we should follow this."

They sat in silence, each lost in their thoughts. Ryan closed his eyes trying to remember the day Anna and her parents drove away. His grandfather had been by his side, telling him it was for the best. That someday, Anna and he would come back together, after *it was all over*. Ryan hadn't thought about that in years. What would be all over? Ryan rubbed his chest. The pain of the loss was as magnified as it had been the day Anna's parents drove away with her. It had always been an ache, but when he really thought of her, his chest hurt with the heartbreak.

He felt Tara squeeze his hand and he opened his eyes to look at her. "You know this isn't your fault?" she whispered. He nodded at her and realized Jake had left the room.

"You look like you are in pain. Talk to me," she said.

"I remember my grandfather standing with me when they drove away. I was crying, heartbroken. She was my best friend. And he said we would come back together when it was all over. I hadn't remembered that in years, but I have no idea what he meant."

"Hang on to that then, that you will see her again." Tara's smile was sad.

"I haven't seen her in years, Tara. It won't change things between you and me. She was my best friend." Ryan didn't feel confident as he said the words, but he knew he had to reassure her somehow.

"We have come into each other lives and had this adventure. And it's been great, but don't think I have any thoughts as to this being a forever thing." Tara's eyes filled with tears as she said the words.

"Stop. Don't do that. You're shutting me out thinking Anna, if we even find her, is going to change anything. Please don't do that."

Tara nodded, but Ryan knew by the look that she had already shut him out.

"I'm going to go for a walk." Tara stood up and headed out of the house.

"You damn fool." Ryan turned to see Jake standing in the door. "Go after her."

Ryan shook his head. "She's already gone."

Jake growled a curse, turning and walked out.

Chapter Thirty-One

Tara walked in the opposite direction of the Holden House. She was gutted knowing Ryan wanted Anna to be back. If they had that strong of a connection, she had no business getting involved with him beyond being friends. She sighed. The sex definitely had complicated things. She should have known better.

"Hey, Tara," Jake yelled to her as he jogged up.

"What are you doing?" She asked.

"Walking with you." He wrapped an arm around her shoulder. "I think you could use a friend right now."

Tara looked at him, and couldn't hold back the tears. "I don't know what I'm doing, Jake."

He pulled her into a full bear hug and held her. "You're being you, and you're confused with all this mess." He held her back so he could see her eyes. "You aren't the only one confused. Know that."

She nodded and sniffled. "Thanks, Jake."

"Come on. There's a great park down the road here with walking trails."

They walked in silence. Tara knew he was giving her

the silence to contemplate things, but she couldn't focus past the fact that Ryan's grandfather had sent Anna and her parents away...paid for them to go away. Why? And how did it tie into the Holden House?

"Do you think hypnosis would work if I tried it? To find my own memories?"

Jake shrugged. "I don't know much about hypnosis, but I suppose it is possible."

"I want to try it."

Jake smiled. "Always so gung-ho to jump into something. I love that adventurous side of you."

Tara smiled. "I didn't used to be this way....at least from what I can remember, I was shyer when I was younger. I don't know. I feel like my gram bringing me here and spurring me to find this boy...who ever that is because I haven't figured that out, but I feel like gram has brought out my adventurous side."

"Well, thank you Gram because I think it is awesome. You show no fear, really. And honestly, the compassion you have for Cecilia despite all she has done has been amazing."

"Well, you are a believer and you know when there is negative paranormal activity, there usually is a reason for their anger."

Jake nodded. He stopped and looked at Tara. "Have you thought of what it means if you are Anna? Cecilia said your grandmother lived in that house. We know Anna's grandmother lived there."

Tara frowned. "I know that's what Cecilia said, but everything in my being tells me that's not right. It's like this gut reaction that is so strong...screaming no."

"This doctor you talked about that treated you after

the fire, which you lost your memory from...can you call him and ask him about hypnosis?"

"I tried contacting him. He passed away last year." Tara shook her head. "I'm afraid there doesn't seem to be any other connections to my parents or my childhood."

They had walked the full loop of the park and were back at Stafford House. Ryan was sitting on the porch waiting for them.

"Everything okay?" he asked, shooting Jake a glare.

Jake grinned at him. "We're great. How are you?"

"Ass," Ryan muttered.

"Did I miss something?" Tara asked.

Both of the men shook their head, grinning at each other. Tara shrugged.

Jake's phone ringing broke the awkwardness. He answered and stepped inside the house. Tara sat down next to Ryan. "Why does it always feel like that one has secrets?" She gestured towards the door where Jake had disappeared.

"Secrets?" Ryan laughed. "The nature of his job. He ensures there is privacy to speak to his clients."

"I thought he had taken some time off." Tara bit her bottom lip. "You know he doesn't have to be here."

"Tell him that. He wants to be here. He's invested now. He could be talking to clients, or to anyone, but it is just his nature to immediately go somewhere private when he takes a call."

Tara nodded. "Are you okay?"

Ryan nodded. "It's been a lot to take in, hasn't it?"

"I think we need to go back to Holden House again. I think there is more there we need to know to finish this puzzle."

"What happened to the envelope we took from there earlier?"

Tara sat up. "I'm pretty sure I put it on the bed. Be right back." Tara ran inside and started up the stairs. She was halfway up when she heard Jake speaking.

"It won't work. Damn it. What do you suggest?"

Tara paused. Who was he talking to? She heard him sign off and jogged up the rest of the stairs. When she got to her room, she stopped in the doorway. The bed was a rumpled mess, remnants of her and Ryan's...what did she call it....sex? She didn't feel it was love making. They weren't at that point. But definitely it was a sexual release from the stress of their encounters earlier that day at Holden House. She pulled the covers up and looked around. She thought she had put the envelope on the bed, but of course it was gone. She got down on her knees and looked under the bed. Nothing. Odd. Where could it have gone?

She sighed and turned toward the bureau. She moved everything and looked behind it. It couldn't have just disappeared. She knew she had it. She had touched it and brought it home. *Gram, where did it go?*

She felt the warmth surround her before she heard her grandmother's voice. *It's too soon. You need to learn more before reading that. You will find it again when it is time.*

Tara stifled a scream of frustration. *Why?*

You are so close.

Tara glanced around the room one more time. She swore softly as she turned toward the door. Tara returned to the porch and Ryan.

"When is Anna's birthday?" she asked suddenly.

"It's in two days, on the 12th." He eyed her. "Why?"

Tara shrugged. "Just wondering. Mine is on the 13th. Guess that eliminates me being Anna." She let out a small laugh.

"Really? Mine's the 12th. Anna and I shared a birthday."

Tara looked at him and smiled. "True soulmates."

"You really have to stop doing that." Ryan reached for her hand. "I'm here with you."

"But let's be honest, you don't know where you would be if you actually knew where Anna was."

"I'd like to think I'm right where I'm supposed to be." Ryan shook his head.

"I want to know why Cecilia states my grandmother lived in the Holden House. I'm not even related to the Holdens."

"Maybe you need to demand answers." Ryan stood. "Let's grab Jake and go back."

"You sure you want to do that?" Tara asked.

"What I want is answers for you. Then maybe we can move on from this and find the peace we had upstairs just earlier."

Tara looked at him. "Peace? Was that what it was, or was it just a release from all the stress?"

Ryan stared at her. He threw up his hands and turned to go inside. "I guess we see it very differently."

Jake came out on the porch. "It doesn't help when you do that."

"What did I do?" Tara asked.

"You are making light of a situation just to push him away. I don't believe for a second you thought you were just releasing steam. I've seen you go for more runs in the past few days than anyone."

Tara sighed. "I need answers and until we have them,

I feel like I'm just a fill in until Anna reappears. And I don't want to feel that way, nor do I want to allow myself to feel for someone that could hurt me in a heartbeat."

"Like Brandon did to Cecilia...that's what you are really saying, right? You believe her crap that because Ryan is a Stafford he is just like his ancestors?"

"I didn't say that," Tara shot back.

"You didn't have to. I have eyes and you two are going to destroy each other with this 'hold each other at bay until we have answers' crap. Hold on to each other instead and get through this *together*." Jake stood up and reached for Tara's hand. "It's the only way either of you are going to survive. Pushing each other away is just what Cecilia wants you to do."

Chapter Thirty-Two

Tara paced the floor outside her bedroom. Jake had found out that hypnosis would not help get her memories back. That it was "unreliable". Unreliable. As if bringing back memories would be more manipulative than erasing them. She bit her bottom lip. She would wear a hole in this carpet if she didn't figure out what she needed to do. More and more little pictures would come to mind, but she didn't recognize them.

Jake came to the bottom of the stairs, watching her. She stopped and stared down at him. "Ryan and I were talking and we think the only way for you to fully get your memories back is to go back to the Holden House again."

"You think Cecilia is going to suddenly let me remember everything," Tara asked, sarcasm laced her words.

Jake chuckled softly. "Maybe not Cecilia. But I think somehow this is all tied to your birthday and the house. Please come give it a try."

Tara nodded and started down the stairs. A warm

breeze enveloped her and she knew her gram was with her. *What do you think, Gram? Please help me.*

I think the young man is right. The answers are in the house. Don't be afraid. You are going to get through this. I'll be with you.

Tara squared her shoulders. At the bottom of the stairs was Jake and Ryan. Both of her knights in shining armor, ready to brave the paranormal world with her. She smiled. "Let's go."

Ryan and Jake shared a glance and then followed her out the door. The walk to the Holden House was quiet. Tara ran through every possible scenario of what could happen. She didn't believe she was Ryan's Anna, but somehow jealously overtook her every time she thought about it. She wanted to be his girl, and yet all of this was such a mess.

They approached the house from the shortcut through the woods and came up the backsteps. Entering the kitchen, Tara leaned against the table. She ran her hand over the grime covering it and willed any memories to come. *Nothing.*

Don't push it. Just let it happen. Her gram's voice in her ear relaxed her. She felt the warmth and moved further into the house. *Go upstairs.*

Tara started upstairs, aware that Jake and Ryan were following her. Neither of them spoke to her, just watched from a distance. Tara ran her fingers along the banister at the top of the stairs. She moved slowly around the open foyer that all the bedrooms opened to. She found herself in front of the room that she thought had been Cecilia's and walked in. She went to the window and looked out. There was a bit of a chill in this room, but she could still feel her grandmother with her. She jumped when the door slammed shut behind her. She heard Jake and Ryan talking outside the door amongst themselves, but they didn't seem too concerned.

"Cecilia? Please let me see you." Tara stood with her back to the window taking in every corner of the room. It was empty...or so it seemed. The chill grew stronger, and yet the warmth on her shoulders let her know her gram was with her.

Why are you here?

Cecilia's voice was icy and Tara involuntarily shivered. "I need answers."

Time is running out.

"How? What time?" Tara demanded.

The end of the 12th will soon be here and you will be no more.

"Stop being cryptic," Tara shouted. "Just say what you mean." Tara felt the warmth spread around her like arms wrapping around her. Instinctively, she wrapped her arms around herself.

Look around.

Tara looked from wall to wall. There was nothing here. "What am I looking for?"

The door opened. Jake poked his head in. "You okay?"

Tara shrugged. "She makes no sense. Tells me to look around. What does that mean?"

"Check out some of the other rooms," Ryan said. He was wandering around the foyer. "What about that room where you saw the dollhouse before?"

Tara turned toward the last room in the hallway. She hadn't been back in this room since the first time she came to the house with Ryan. It had been a child's room. The dollhouse stood against the wall and she went over to it. She picked up a tiny couch that was in the house's living room. She held it for a moment with her eyes closed before she put it back. She moved to the closet and opened the door. There was a few dresses hanging and Tara reached out to touch them. Warmth surrounded her and she pulled one of them off their hanger and held it close.

The flash came and she sank to her knees. A birthday cake. It had a rainbow and a unicorn on it. A girl was giggling at it, clapping her hands. The picture faded as quickly as it came. *Who was that, Gram?*

There was no reply from her grandmother, but the warmth surrounded her once more. Tara clung to the dress, willing another picture to come...something to give her answers. Tears welled in her eyes. A chill filled the room.

Cecilia. What do you want?

Child, I want you to know what is happening. You need to know the truth that has been hidden from you all these years.

"What truth?" Tara spoke out loud, turning on the floor to face the room. She continued to hold the dress.

It will come to you.

Tara stood and hung the dress back up. She closed her eyes and exhaled slowly. Getting upset was not going to help. The door snapped shut and Tara went to it. She pulled on the handle, but it would not open. She could hear Ryan outside the door.

"Knock it off, Cecilia."

Although silence filled the air, with her hand on the door, Tara could feel the icy air coming from the other side. "Jake? Ryan? Are you guys alright?"

"It's okay, Tara," Jake's voice was calming. "Cecilia apparently is trying to get through to Ryan."

"Get through about what?" she asked.

"I don't know."

Tara heard what she assumed was Ryan gasping for air. "Ryan?" she yelled, yanking on the door handle.

"I'm okay," Ryan's voice was hoarse. "Cecilia, you can't stop me."

You will not have her. She should have died long ago, but know it will be in front of you.

"Who should have died?"

Anna.

Ryan gasped in pain. "Anna? Where is she?"

The door handle turned violently in Tara's hand and she was able to open the door. Ryan was on the floor with Jake leaning over him.

"What happened?" She rushed to Ryan's side.

Ryan sat up. "Felt like an icicle going through me. I'm fine."

Jake helped him to his feet. "Keep looking, Tara."

"I'm not leaving Ryan like this. We need to get him out of here. She won't hurt me, but obviously she wants to hurt him."

"I'm not leaving you in here alone. I'm not convinced she won't hurt you too," Ryan said.

"Gram is here. She will protect me," Tara said. "Please Ryan, please go outside."

"No. I'm not leaving you." He looked around. "You hear that Cecilia? I'm not leaving her."

Another door slammed behind them. Tara laughed. "Obviously she is not happy with you."

"Let's keep looking."

Tara looked at both of the men. "I saw a flash in that room. I was holding a dress that was hanging in the closet and saw this birthday cake. I don't know whose it was though."

Jake gave her a prod. "Go back in there. See what else you can find."

Tara nodded and moved back into the room. She moved to the bureau against the far wall. It was an antiqued piece of furniture that had a round mirror on top of it. She stood before it and looked at herself in the mirror. It was covered with grime and her image was obstructed. She peered and leaned in to get a closer look and she saw a young girl with a woman standing behind her. The woman was braiding the girl's hair. The girl petite and was probably only four or five years old. Her nose was covered with freckles. Tara squinted into the mirror. She didn't recognize the woman behind the girl.

Tara felt fingers run through her hair and she closed her eyes. She envisioned her grandmother's hand running through her hair as if she was the little girl in the mirror. She opened her eyes and found herself looking at her own reflection. The little girl was gone and Tara stared at the mirror. She searched her own face. She had never had freckles. She had always wanted them. She remembered thinking as a child that girls with freckles were the cutest girls around.

Open your mind, Gram's voice whispered in her ear. *Don't just search with your eyes. Listen to what your heart is telling you.*

Tara shook her head. What did that mean? She looked down at the bureau. The top was empty and she pulled open the top drawer. Inside she saw a small stuffed bunny. It was a light brown and had blue eyes. Tara picked it up and held it. Suddenly she saw a girl holding it, sobbing into it. Tara could feel the pain the girl felt. Her heart broke at the sight of it. The girl was inconsolable and the woman appeared again, wrapping the girl in her arms. Just like the warmth of her gram's arms around her.

Is that me, Grams?

Yes. You were devastated.

Tara closed her eyes, trying to hold on to the memory. She didn't recognize the girl. She was five or six years old. *I kept the bunny for you. Your parents didn't let you take anything with you when you left.*

"Why?"

You had to start fresh.

"I don't understand," Tara cried. Tara looked down at the bunny and tried to envision that memory she had just seen. It didn't feel like a memory of hers at all, but instead like watching a stranger in a movie. She kept holding the bunny and turned to leave the room.

She got to the foyer and found Ryan and Jake sitting on the floor waiting for her. "Apparently this was mine. I don't remember anything."

Ryan sat up. "Anna had one like that. She carried it everywhere."

"I don't think I'm Anna. You said it yourself; her birthday is different than mine," Tara adamantly said. Frustration laced her words.

Thud.

Tara turned toward the room with the yellow wallpaper. She stood, gripping the bunny, and walked toward the room. As soon as she crossed the threshold, the temperature dropped considerably. Cecilia.

Still not understanding. Time is running out, child. Cecilia's laugh sent a shiver down Tara's back and she stopped. She looked around. This room had been empty, but on the floor now sat the envelope that Tara could swear she had put on her bed. She reached for it. She forced herself to pick it up, although the iciness bit her fingers and she cried out. She turned and returned to the foyer.

Jake took the envelope from her and opened it. A cold breeze knocked it from his hands. *Hers,* Cecilia's voice hissed as the envelope dropped to the floor.

Tara reached for it once more. She slid out the contents and placed them on the floor in front of the three of them. There were two birth certificates. One for Anna Tara Holden, date of birth May 12, 1992. The other for Tara Shetfield, date of birth May 13, 1992. Tara glanced to Ryan and Jake.

Chapter Thirty-Three

TARA HAD PICKED UP THE BIRTH CERTIFICATES AND GONE downstairs to the kitchen. She had told Jake and Ryan she needed a bit of space to just think. They guys had stayed upstairs as Ryan was hoping to *talk* with Cecilia some more.

He didn't have long to wait as she made her appearance as soon as he walked into the room where Tara had found the bunny. She slammed the door behind him and he turned. For the first time, he saw an angry woman in front of him dressed in a long blue dress.

"Cecilia."

Go away. You don't belong in this room.

"Why? What are you hiding from me?"

"Ryan, dude, you okay?" Jake yelled from outside the door.

"Fine. No worries," Ryan answered.

You should worry. You have less than 48 hours before she's gone.

"Are you going to kill her?" Ryan baited.

I won't need to. She can't outrun the curse that came when I died.

"When you killed yourself you mean. You did this?"

There has never been another female in the Holden family before that has lived past 25. She won't either.

"Is Tara really Anna?"

She needs to learn the truth herself. You can't love her. It's not in the Stafford nature.

"Not true. I love her with all my heart. I want what you always wanted...a home with her, a family with her."

With whom? Tara or Anna? You may once have loved Anna, but that love doesn't translate to Tara.

"Of course it does."

Neither is your soulmate.

"Is that what this is about? You think one of them should be my soulmate?" Ryan spun around in the room. It was Anna's old room. "I always had a connection with Anna and probably always will. But there is a connection with Tara too. And I'm not searching for Anna. I want Tara to be happy."

She needs to find her soulmate before her birthday.

"Are you saying that will save her life?"

Get out. The door swung open and the vision disappeared. Ryan stood there looking at the open door trying to wrap his head around the conversation he had with Cecilia. The curse. Female from the Holden family dies without their soulmate. He stepped out of the room and Jake was standing there waiting. He filled him in on the conversation.

"Shit. What now?" Jake asked.

"It's up to Tara. Everything relies on her getting her memories back."

Jake looked at him. "You think she's Anna."

Ryan shrugged. "I don't know, but it doesn't matter. I love Tara. And she is the one I want to be with."

"Well, it's about time you came to that realization." Jake clapped him on the back. "About time."

They both went in search of Tara only to find the kitchen empty. They split up and started searching the main floor of the house. Nothing. All the doors were open and rooms were empty. Secret passages were closed with no indication she had gone that way. They reconvened in the kitchen. Jake walked to the door and looked out. Tara stood at the edge of the woods looking into it. With her back to them, she was oblivious that they had been searching for her.

Ryan started out to go to her, but Jake put a hand on his arm. "Wait. Let her work things out. She needs to process. My guess is her grams is with her."

Ryan sighed. "Do you know how hard it is to stand back and just watch her struggle."

Jake smiled. "Yeah, man. You aren't the only one that cares about her."

Ryan raised an eyebrow at him.

Jake laughed. "Not like you, trust me. But she has become a good friend and I want to see her happy and live a long life."

Ryan looked at the papers on the table. There was the two birth certificates, but also a letter that Tara must have found. He picked it up and read:

My dearest,

You've been gone only a day and I miss you dearly. You were like a fixture in this house, you and Ryan. Ryan has also been missing you. He has been here twice already to see if I have heard from you and asking where you went. I couldn't tell him as your parents didn't want me to know where you would be. They were afraid I would come see you. My child, my heart is broken to not see you grown up. I only hope that if you are reading this, you have made your way back home and I wish I could be here with you.

You must know your heart and accept whatever you feel. Don't fight it. There isn't time for that. If you have made it past your 25th birthday, then you have survived the worst. Know that. This house is yours. May your love cleanse the hall of all sadness.

All my love, Grams

Ryan dropped the letter and looked out at Tara. She was still facing the woods and he longed to just go to her and find out what she was thinking.

"Don't do it," Jake's voice cut through his thoughts and he turned to see Jake watching him. "Let her have the space."

"If everything Cecilia and this letter states is true, then she doesn't have much time. Her birthday is in two days."

"Do you think it is true?" Jake asked.

"I don't know, but do you really want to take that chance."

Jake shrugged. "If it is a curse, there really isn't anything we can do to break it. It's all on Tara, or Anna."

Chapter Thirty-Four

TARA FACED THE WOODS. TEARS WERE STREAMING DOWN HER face as she stood there wondering what to make of it all. There had been a letter with the birth certificates. It wasn't addressed to anyone other than *My Dearest*. Was it for Anna or for her? Deep in her gut, she now knew she was Anna and that letter was hers whether she was Tara or Anna. Her grandmother, Grams. The woman who had gotten her through everything, the woman Tara thought she had never met before, but had only had conversations with on the phone. The woman who had brought her to this place...her home...and back to Ryan.

That brought heartache to her. Ryan. How hard this will be for him. She knew she still had a connection as Anna with him, but Anna was gone. That girl had died years ago when they took her memories away. Tara was here now and how would Ryan feel about that? She wasn't sure if his feelings were the same for Tara as they were for Anna. He had been so adamant about finding out what happened to Anna, that Tara wasn't sure if he recognized that in some warped way he had made her feel like she was second fiddle to Anna. It shouldn't matter if they were one and the same.

Tara wiped at her tears. *Grams, I don't know what to do with this information. How do I survive this?*

You are a Holden, my dear. You have the inner strength, always have. Holden women are strong. Even Cecilia. We all have our breaking point, but this isn't yours.

Tara heard the words and the love that came through with them. She was a strong woman. She had survived losing both her parents, obviously losing her childhood, and now finding out she was someone else than who she thought she was. She had this. She turned and faced the house. Wow. This house was her house.

Jake and Ryan were on the backsteps waiting for her. She was so grateful that they had given her the space she needed to breathe and process. She smiled at them and walked toward the house. Her eyes looked at the house differently now. She remembered being here. The yard filled with flowerbeds where her and Ryan played hide-n-seek, and picnicked with her Grams. She smiled and looked up. Cecilia was in the upstairs window watching her. Tara stopped and stared. Could she break this curse that Cecilia had started all those years ago?

She started walking faster toward the house. "There's a lot to talk about, but first I have more questions for Cecilia. Stay here, please?" It came out a question, but she begged them silently to understand she needed them to stay downstairs.

They both nodded and didn't say a word. She walked past them into the house. When she arrived at the staircase, she stood at the bottom, looking up. This is where it all started. Cecilia had hung herself off this banister over this foyer. Tara wiped a lone tear away. The poor woman had reached her breaking point like Grams said, but she wasn't going to push Tara to that point. Tara strode up the stairs. "Cecilia?" She went to Cecilia's doorway and looked in.

Cecilia stood at the window, as clear as she had ever been to Tara. When she turned to face Tara, tears shone on her translucent cheeks. Tara stepped into the room. "Cecilia, I'm sorry for the heartbreak you suffered. I truly am, but you have to let go of this."

It's not my choice. Only you can change it. Cecilia took a step closer to Tara and reached her hand out. Tara reached out for her and although she couldn't feel anything but a chill when their hands met, Tara noticed it wasn't as frigid as before. *I watched over you as a child, but when you and that boy had such a bond, I couldn't let it continue. I never meant to hurt you then.*

"You were the reason I fell in the hole?"

Cecilia nodded. *I had scared you in the house and you ran. You weren't watching. I could see you fall in from my window.*

"I forgive you."

Cecilia shook her head. *It's not enough.*

"What else do I have to do?" Tara asked.

You have to have what I wanted. It has to be rock solid, your soulmate. I cannot break it. When I took my life that night, Brandon's relief of being rid of me bonded the curse to the house. It broke me, his lack of love for me. My false sense of him being my soulmate has cursed the female Holdens to death unless they find their soulmate before they turn twenty-five.

"Wait. How does Brandon control this?"

217

He wasn't my soulmate. He broke me and only someone who can break past that will survive.

"I don't even know if I believe in soulmates." Tara shook her head in frustration. "And I have only until my birthday, which apparently now is a day earlier than I thought it was."

Cecilia smiled. It was an odd smile, one that Tara couldn't tell was of sadness or malice. *You are so much like your grandmother. She was fierce with me at times. We lived together quite comfortably most of the time, especially after you had left. I knew this day would come though and that you would be back here before you died.*

"I have so many questions."

Cecilia shook her head. *I cannot answer anything else. You must find it within yourself, the rest of the answers.* Cecilia started to slip away and Tara heard her last words. *Don't let me hurt you.*

Tara looked around the room. She slid down to the floor and leaned against the door. She pulled her knees to her and wrapped her arms around them. Soulmates. It wasn't a thing, was it? She never believed in that sort of thing. Though remembering now her connection with Ryan, were soulmates just connected friends whose bond never broke. What if it wasn't romantic? She shook her head. It had to be if it was going to break a curse where Cecilia had killed herself over a lack of love from her husband. She cringed. She loved Ryan. She knew she did the moment she gave herself freely to him. She would not have done that with any man she didn't truly love. There had been a rawness and vulnerability that was far more than just 'release sex' as she had tried to blame it on. Instead she felt the love within her for Ryan and it was not just 'sex'.

She sighed. She needed to tell Ryan this and she hoped those words would break the curse. Was it just that simple? Say *I love you* and suddenly everything would be right in the world again. No. It had to be reciprocated by Ryan, and that is where the real question mark was in this equation.

Chapter Thirty-Five

TARA HAD JUMPED IN THE SHOWER AS SOON AS THEY GOT home. She planned on talking to Ryan later, but needed to gather her thoughts. There was no way to do this easily. She found him on the porch when she came downstairs.

"Where's Jake?"

Ryan glanced up as she sat down next to him. "He decided to take off for a bit and let us talk."

Tara nodded. "You read the letter."

"Yes." Ryan waited.

"I remember things now. I remember us as kids. I know I am Anna, but I'm not. Does that make sense?"

Ryan got up from the chair and went to sit on the railing so he was facing her. "I get it. Those memories are gone, although you may remember some of them, there is no emotional connection with them. It doesn't matter, Tara."

"But it does. If the curse has to be broken by Anna, I can't do that."

"Yes, you can. Because Tara is Anna and Anna is Tara.

You are Tara and that is the reality of it. But biologically, you are Anna and have the power to break the curse."

"I don't," Tara scowled.

"What do you mean?"

"It's not up to me. According to Cecilia, I have to find my soulmate." She shrugged. "I'm not even sure I believe in soulmates."

Ryan smiled. "You want my two cents?"

"Of course."

"We have been soulmates since we were little, running around your grandmother's yard. We were connected, which is why it was so hard when you left. But don't you see, you were brought back here for a reason. A reason that brought you to stay here in my house, and I was suddenly brought home to be here with you and help you solve this. We are still connected. Don't tell me you haven't felt it? From the moment I met you, Tara, there has been this strong connection that drew me to you. I have wanted you from the moment I laid eyes on you when you insisted I call the cops ,on me being in my own house." He chuckled.

Tara laughed. "Yes, but friendship is not a connection that is going to break this curse."

Ryan jumped off the railing and knelt in front of her, gripping her hands. "Do you think I would have allowed sex to happen with someone I considered just a friend? Tara, I fell head over heels in love with you that moment you interrogated the policeman, and I've been trying to figure it out all this time. How was it possible to be this connected to you? To want to be with you, body and soul. I want with you what Cecilia never got to have...a loving relationship, eventually a family of our own. I love you, Tara."

Tara stared at him. Her heart fluttered at the words he said and she leaned forward to kiss him. "I love you," she whispered.

They moved to the swing where they could sit side by side. Holding hands, they talked about the years they were apart and more and more of Tara's memories started filling in. It was like the affirmation of love had opened the secret door that had held those memories for years. She was overwhelmed with it all, but talked and talked about how she had cried for weeks after they moved, missing Ryan. Her parents hadn't let her talk to her grandmother. It wasn't until after the so-called fire when she lost her memories that suddenly she had a grandmother that called her almost every day to check on her.

She realized now there had been no fire. She remembered the hypnosis where the doctor had shut her memories away. She had been told she would remember when the time was right. And suddenly the time was right. She had a birthday in a little over 24 hours, and suddenly she didn't know if she was going to live or die by the end of that day.

She leaned her head on Ryan's shoulder and closed her eyes. A peace had settled over her and she knew that it didn't matter what happened by her birthday's end. She had found love, and in this moment, that was all that mattered.

Chapter Thirty-Six

IT WAS MAY 12TH. RYAN AND TARA'S BIRTHDAY. TARA LOOKED at herself in the mirror and thought about the oddness of the situation. Her birthday after all these years really being on the 12th instead of the 13th. She wondered if her parents planned that especially so they could celebrate if she made it through another year. It was a morbid thought, but one she realized she would have done to her own daughter if her life had depended on it.

She went downstairs to find Jake and Ryan waiting for her. Jake held a bag.

"What's that?"

"We're going to celebrate in your new home."

Tara laughed. It was not official yet. She hadn't wanted to claim the house until after her birthday. If she was still here, she would take over the house. If not, the town could have the house. She still wasn't sure if the curse had been broken, but she was hopeful. Ryan and she had spent a quiet past 24 hours reminiscing, filling each other in on all the details they would have shared over the years if they had been in contact, and talking about their love for each other.

They walked into the kitchen at the Holden House. Tara noticed the kitchen table was spotless and set with clean plates. "Who cleaned?"

Jake grinned. "Happy Birthday, guys."

Tara kissed him on the cheek. "Thank you."

Jake unpacked the bag of a cake and a knife. A noise upstairs stopped them. Tara looked at Ryan. She had hoped Cecilia would be gone to indicate the curse was broken. Her breath caught as she took a step towards the front hall and the stairway.

At the bottom of the stairs, Tara looked up. There was Cecilia standing at the top of the stairs. "What happens now?" Tara asked.

Happy birthday, Anna and Ryan.

Tara nodded and looked at Ryan. He had heard her also. They watched as Cecilia floated down the stairs as she descended towards them. Tara felt Ryan brace himself next to her and his fingers intertwined with hers. Tara felt a soft brush against her cheek as Cecilia kissed her.

Be happy. You found him and I know he will do better than Brandon did. Be happy and know your daughters will never face the same curse. Cecilia turned towards Ryan. *You proved your love for her. When we spoke the other day, I never felt such love from my husband that you showed for your soulmate. Never let that change, Ryan.*

"I won't. Thank you, Cecilia."

It was not my choice. The Staffords had the power all along to do better. It was always in your power to determine if you loved her enough to save her.

In an instant, she was gone. The chill was no longer

part of the house. Tara looked around. It was brighter, despite the dingy windows. She looked up at the banister and imagined the sadness as Cecilia had taken her life. It had been the start of a century long curse that fortunately had only effected female Holden women. And Tara had been the first to survive it.

She turned towards Ryan and Jake. "Let's have cake."

About the Author

Emma Leigh Reed, originally from New Hampshire, now resides in Tennessee. She has fond memories of the Maine coastline and incorporates the ocean into all her books. She has three grown children and is enjoying her empty nest. Her life has been touched and changed by her son's autism - she views life through a very different lens than before he was born. Growing up as an avid reader, it was only natural for Emma Leigh to turn to creating the stories for others to enjoy. Emma Leigh continues to learn through her children's strength and abilities that pushes her to go outside her comfort zone on a regular basis. She teaches English at a local college. She is the author of romantic suspense, women's fiction, paranormal romance, crime thrillers, and has co-authored children's books.

For more information please visit emmaleighreed.com

www.ingramcontent.com/pod-product-compliance
Lightning Source LLC
Chambersburg PA
CBHW060634260626
47161CB00008B/2891